'I believe i
which is th
that can he
said. 'What's your problem with that?'

They glared at each other, and she watched Jake's eyes narrow.

'Hocus pocus, Poppy. Natural doesn't automatically mean safe. There is no scientific proof that these methods work—and I think it's dangerous. When something goes wrong it's my *conventional medicine* that's going to save them.'

By the time he finished his tirade his voice had risen.

'I'm not deaf, Jake. On the surface, your arguments are old school and nothing I can't demolish. But there's something deeper and more personal in this explosion of emotion. What experiences have you had with alternative therapies?' She gentled her voice. She didn't want to cause him pain. Wasn't even sure of the reaction she might get, let alone the fallout—but it was too late.

Fiona McArthur is Australian and lives with her husband and five sons on the Mid-North Coast of New South Wales. Her interests are writing, reading, playing tennis, e-mail and discovering the fun of computers—of course that's when she's not watching the boys play competition cricket, football or tennis. She loves her work as a part-time midwife in a country hospital, facilitates antenatal classes and enjoys the company of young mothers in a teenage pregnancy group.

Now that her youngest son has started school Fiona has more time for writing and is looking forward to the challenge of improving her craft. DELIVERING LOVE is her first novel.

DELIVERING LOVE

BY

FIONA McARTHUR

MILLS & BOON®

To my Dad—my first hero.

First published in Great Britain 2000
Harlequin Mills & Boon Limited,
Eton House, 18-24 Paradise Road, Richmond, Surrey TW9 1SR

ISBN 0 263 82292 3

Set in Times Roman 10½ on 12 pt.
03-0201-45224

Printed and bound in Spain
by Litografia Rosés, S.A., Barcelona

CHAPTER ONE

'CAESAREAN birth, seventeen-ten,' the scout nurse intoned. Everyone glanced at the clock as the baby was delivered into the world. Nobody spoke. The theatre staff at Midcoast Hospital, New South Wales, were too busy willing the baby to move.

The child lay tinged with blue and still, across his mother's green-draped stomach.

Come on, Baby, Poppy McCrae urged silently as she moved into action. This was why she was here. She knew how resilient babies were once they had oxygen and the stimulation of the outside world.

Her gloved fingers directed the tiny suction tube to gently clear his mouth and nose as Dr Gates clamped and severed the ropy link between the baby and his mother.

Poppy gathered the tiny human to her chest and carried him to the resuscitation trolley. How he responded in the next five minutes would indicate his oxygen depletion.

Her elbow knocked the clock timer to keep track of time since birth and she positioned him on his back with his head towards her. She briskly rubbed the infant's damp skin with a warmed towel. Sometimes, towelling would be enough to stimulate a baby to breathe. His little limbs wobbled slackly with her movements and Poppy winced. Twenty seconds since birth.

She reached for the stethoscope and listened for his heartbeat, heard the newborn's slow steady beating in her ears and exhaled in relief. A sluggish beat was much better than no beat at all.

Placing the mask firmly over his nose and mouth, she gently squeezed oxygen into the tiny lungs with short puffs from the bag. Poppy nodded slightly at the way his chest rose and fell as she squeezed the bag.

One minute since birth. It felt like ten. His heart rate was better at just under a hundred beats a minute. She glanced up at the scrub-room window. *Still* nobody there. She frowned. Where was this new paediatrician?

'Do it, Baby. Wake up and smell everybody sweating.' She rubbed the infant again and continued puffing oxygen through the mask, noting the faint improvement in his skin colour.

'You're a dawdler, but you're working on it. Good boy.' She patted him.

The operating-theatre doors whooshed open and Poppy looked up briefly in relief. A tall figure, masked and gowned, strode over to the resuscitaire.

'Dr Sheppard. Paediatrician. How long since birth?'

The previous week's speculation about him was unimportant now and she glanced at the timer ticking away. 'Two minutes, Doctor.' They still didn't know why the baby had become distressed during labour, and Poppy prayed there was no birth defect causing the problem.

She swapped places so he could stand at the baby's head. 'Slow foetal heart rate since admission and decreased foetal movement. Stunned at birth. No respiratory effort as yet, although pinking up slightly with bagging. Heart rate just under a hundred now.'

Poppy kept her gaze on the baby's chest as it rose and fell with each squeeze of the black rubber bag.

'How long was the labour and how much pethidine did the mother have?'

'Less than four hours before the midwife noticed a sudden change in foetal heartbeat. As for the other…' Poppy smiled at the memory of the baby's earth mother and looked up at him '…we don't use pain relief like pethidine very often here. The only drugs on board come from the anaesthetic. The baby was supposed to be born at home.'

She saw Dr Sheppard narrow his eyes and grimace. Great. She gritted her teeth. He's not sympathetic to home births. She'd have to work on that. Later.

'Hmm,' was all he said. 'Now, Baby, we'll pop a little tube down your throat to help you breathe for a few minutes, and if you're very good I'll take it out again shortly.'

He listened to the infant's chest and then took over the bagging so that Poppy could prepare the equipment. As she placed each object on top of the trolley she couldn't help noticing how gentle his large hands were as he handled the newborn.

His voice rumbled on a deeper note as he spoke to the baby, and Poppy felt as if a cool breeze had somehow eddied into Theatre and blown across her neck. She shrugged off the thought that the cadences in his speech were niggling her as familiar, but she had to admit he had a great voice.

Not since her big city hospital training had Poppy felt so attuned during resuscitation, and she wordlessly placed the laryngoscope into his upturned palm. As she watched the diminutive patient lie flaccidly under his care, she sensed the anxiety of the other staff. There was none of the usual conversation.

The first signs of response started to appear. Poppy welcomed the lightening of weight in her own chest as, with each puff of the bag, the baby's skin colour washed pinker from the oxygen. With the tiniest movements, the baby began to twitch and move.

Go for it, Baby! Poppy urged the little boy on in her mind. His plump hands clenched and the tiny toes spread as if in answer.

Relief washed over her like incoming surf. His little face grimaced and his chest fluttered as he struggled to breathe for himself.

Poppy sighed with relief. Any second now. She positioned the oxygen mask back over the baby's face as Dr Sheppard removed the tube to allow the infant to breathe for himself.

The baby gasped and coughed. Then came the most beautiful sound in the world. He cried.

Poppy's eyes misted and she looked up to meet those of the man beside her.

It was then that she fully took in the height, the forehead and those vivid blue eyes. It wasn't just the voice that was familiar. For a moment she doubted her own sanity until common sense stepped in.

That man was dead!

She looked again and saw a different man beneath the green theatre attire. Similar but not the same. She shook her head and relegated another thought to later.

Refocussing on the crying baby, a smile spread from deep inside her. To hell with it. The baby was fine, they'd done a good job and life was great. She was glad they had a new paediatrician, even though doctors weren't her favourite people. She smiled from her heart at this tall, skilled doctor standing beside her. He looked back and for a moment it seemed as if he, too, had been moved by the moment until his gaze hardened and he seemed to look right through her. Poppy shrugged and looked away.

The baby was roaring loudly now and she bundled him up in warm bunny rugs while keeping the oxygen mask tucked near his mouth. She watched Dr Sheppard gently pat the little boy to soothe him. He seemed to genuinely care about his little patient. Maybe he was one of the good guys.

All across Theatre, breaths were expelled and talk broke out.

'I think everyone needs some oxygen after that. Well done,' Dr Gates called out. He added, satisfaction clearly evident in his voice, 'We've found the culprit, a true knot in the umbilical cord that pulled tighter during labour. Your young man was running out of time in there.'

Dr Sheppard looked across at the surgeon. 'That answers a lot of questions. I'd say your decision not to wait was a good one. Baby responded well and I can't foresee any problems.' He looked back at Poppy and frowned.

Poppy's own brows drew together at the expression on the new doctor's face. What was eating him? She mentally shrugged. Did she really care? 'Are you happy enough with the baby for me to transfer him back to the ward?'

She watched the scowl smooth away in front of her eyes. She sighed and hoped he wasn't going to be another one of those doctors with unpredictable moods.

'Yes, Baby's fine. I'll come with you and talk to the father. I gather he's the poor chap nail-biting out in the corridor.'

Dr Gates looked up from his suturing. 'Thank you for coming at such short notice, Dr Sheppard. I know you don't start until tomorrow but in the country everyone knows your comings and goings. You can't hide from us.' He laughed, the way only really chubby men could, and everyone joined in as they watched him wobble with mirth.

'By the way, the very efficient midwife at your side is Sister McCrae. Sister McCrae—Dr Sheppard.' He chuckled as the two looked at each other and then away. 'Thanks again. Midcoast won't always call you in at dinnertime.'

'Not a problem.' Dr Sheppard nodded at Poppy and they manoeuvred the trolley carrying the baby out of the theatre. They paused, before pushing open the swing doors, and threw their masks and theatre gowns into the bins provided. The baby was so snugly wrapped that only his wrinkled face poked out of the mound of blankets. Poppy stroked his cheek. His skin felt like silk against her fingers. Newborn babies never ceased to fill her with wonder. Once she would have given anything to have been able to have one.

As they pushed open the external doors from the theatre the child's father jumped up from his seat and rushed towards them.

'Congratulations, Luke!' Poppy said. 'Sheila's fine and so is your son.'

'It's a boy!' he whooped, but quickly sobered, or as much as the grin on his face would allow. 'You're sure they're both OK?'

'This is Dr Sheppard. He's the paediatrician and he can tell you all about it…' Poppy's voice dwindled away as Luke fastened his eyes on the other man.

She, too, turned to study his face properly for the first time. The bottom seemed to drop out of her stomach. He was a stunner. In the corridor lighting, the lines of his cheekbones made his face seem almost harsh. His full bottom lip hinted at sensuality and softened the strength of his powerful jaw. It affected Poppy in a way she wasn't prepared for. Her own lips tightened in denial. She wouldn't even think about it!

Still she found herself drawn to his eyes. That vivid blue of the sea on a sunny day. There was that memory again. She knew who he reminded her of now. She'd only seen eyes of that colour once before—and then they'd been outlined by very sparse eyebrows. She'd kissed that man's brow goodbye two weeks before he'd died. She shivered at the eerie feeling it left her with.

The men were talking and she couldn't help noticing how broad and reassuring Dr Sheppard looked in his theatre trousers and V-necked top. A few stray black tendrils of chest hair poked out brazenly around his neckline and the fabric stretched tautly across the widest chest she'd seen in town for a while. She gulped and tried not to stare.

A gentle pulsing warmth started low in her stomach as she watched him absently stroke the bundled baby on the trolley. What would it feel like to be cradled in those strong arms? He'd draw women like kids to a sweets jar.

She winced as if hit by a wet flannel. Just like her ex-husband. The snake.

She glared at his tall frame. Typical. See how easily Dr Sheppard instilled trust in the father, she warned herself. She'd seen what a smooth talker could do once before.

'Thanks, Doc. Thanks, Sister.' Luke could hardly stand still in his excitement and relief. 'I'm off to the phones.' He sped off down the corridor, more excited than if he'd picked the winner in the Melbourne Cup.

Poppy seized gratefully on the break in her thoughts and helped steer the trolley through to the neonatal nursery.

'I'll do a thorough check before he goes into the crib, Sister.' Poppy nodded and unwrapped the infant.

She watched Dr Sheppard check the infant. She had to admire the way his concentration focussed totally on the baby as he carefully assessed him from every angle.

When he was finished, he closed the tiny circular door with a gentle click. Poppy chalked up another point for him. She'd seen so many doctors snap the door shut, oblivious to the arm-flinging agitation of the baby within. She could work with this guy, she decided.

Then he spoiled it. 'I can't believe people put their children at risk by having babies at home. If I had my choice I'd ban it.' He shook his head as he stared at the little fellow now resting comfortably in his artificial womb.

Poppy's mouth dropped open. 'Excuse me?'

Dr Sheppard glanced up at her measuringly. 'You don't agree, Sister?'

Cold blue eyes met militant green ones.

Poppy's gaze didn't waver. 'No, I don't agree.'

'So convince me!' He didn't actually put his hands on his hips but he might as well have.

You bet I will, buddy. Poppy smiled sweetly. 'My success would depend on whether you're open to reasonable argument or whether your mind is already made up, Doctor.'

There was no answering smile and he spoke with sudden coldness. '*Touché.* I don't like your chances. Maybe another day.' He saluted her. 'Thank you, Sister.'

Poppy shivered. Perhaps he wouldn't be so easy to convince. It wasn't just the right of the parent to choose the place of birth that she wanted to convince him of. Instinctively, she felt it would be hugely important to avoid any problems with her beliefs in midwifery. He could set her cause back two years if his demands were unreasonable.

Twenty minutes later, back in her usual uniform, Poppy could feel her feet dragging. She rotated her neck and shoulders to ease out any stiffness from the long day as she walked over to the crib.

'Bye, Baby. We couldn't help a true knot in your cord.' She shivered at the closeness of tragedy. 'It's a shame about your mummy's poor old tummy but you're a lucky little boy.'

'So how was our new paediatrician, Poppy?' Sandy, the other midwife, pulled a butterscotch sweet out of her pocket and handed it to Poppy.

'Thanks.' Poppy untwisted the prize out of its wrapping and popped it into her mouth, rolling her eyes as the sweetness hit her tongue.

Poppy put her hand over her mouth as she crunched the butterscotch with her teeth. Sandy put her hands over her ears and the two women grinned at each other.

'Sorry. I needed that. I haven't eaten for about six hours.' She pointed at the baby and answered Sandy's question. 'Well, I was pretty glad to see him, with the baby so stunned at birth, and he puts a tube in very well.' She rolled the sweet wrapper in her hands thoughtfully. 'He's got that calmness the really experienced neonatal guys have so that everything seems to go smoothly with no stress. Very easy to work with.'

'Hooray, you've said something good about a doctor finally.' Sandy pretended to do a Red Indian war dance around the room.

Poppy glared at her. 'I like Dr Gates.'

'He's as round as butter and married with six kids. He's safe to like. Besides, he finally agreed with your complementary therapies. But this guy is *young* and Dr Gates says he's *single.*'

'Yeah, but I've got a bad feeling about how open his mind is. Also, he's against a mother choosing the place of birth.' Poppy rubbed her eyes and stretched her neck again. 'Still, I suppose if everyone had their babies at home we'd be out of a job.'

Sandy frowned. 'Don't worry about him now. It's been a long day for you and pressure's on when a baby's not responding.'

'It's OK, Sandy. I'm thinking that at least, having him here, we won't have to book as many high-risk women into the base hospital.' She stared dreamily at a rosy vision of babies and mothers filling the nursery.

Sandy shook her head. 'What I don't get is why such a qualified guy would come here.'

Poppy sniffed. 'Why wouldn't he come here? We have the best beaches on the North Coast and we're close to about five national parks.'

'Yeah, right, Poppy. Not everyone wants to tramp through slippery gullies to look at some hundred-year-old forest giant covered in green velvet.' Sandy rolled her eyes.

Poppy wasn't listening. 'Hopefully, more women will come back to having their babies at Midcoast.' She looked around at the freshly painted walls and the modern equipment.

'I love this place and we fought hard for the birthing suites. It infuriates me that there's no guarantee the ward will stay open if the birth numbers keep falling.' She crossed her fingers superstitiously. 'Help is here if they need it, but we're finally offering our clients non-medical forms of pain relief, with great results. People are starting to chose Midcoast for those reasons. We don't want another doctor to scare them away by being negative. We'll just have to convince him that, while it has its place, conventional medicine isn't always necessary.'

She shrugged her shoulders wearily and waved at the baby again.

'I've had it. Bye, little one.' She blew a kiss at the crib. 'See you tomorrow afternoon, Sandy.' With her bag in one hand and helmet and keys in the other, she headed thoughtfully out of the door. Poppy's red motor scooter was no Harley-Davidson but it meant she didn't have to walk home in the dark tonight.

Pushing open the external door, she almost collided with Dr Sheppard who was leaping up the stairs three at a time. Poppy stepped back out of his way but stopped when he put out his hand.

'Hello again, Sister.' He glanced at her helmet. 'It's dark. I'll walk you to your, ah…bike?'

This tall, muscular man, vaulting the stairs, had knocked her mentally off balance. Poppy forced down the butterflies in her stomach and managed a noncommittal nod. But she smiled to herself at a reaction she hadn't enjoyed in a while. Hormones.

What was that thing about adrenalin she'd learnt? It warmed your skin with increased blood flow and accelerated your heartbeat. This guy must trigger her adrenalin. And he'd know it, too. The thought steadied her. She'd had the impression he hadn't even liked her. Strangely, she wasn't tired any more.

Poppy walked beside him the short distance to the road. 'Why do you want to walk me to my bike?' She tilted her head up at him, unable to resist. 'Did you want to hear why some home births are a good thing? How important it is that if these parents come to us in a crisis situation we shouldn't judge them?'

His face showed it was the last thing he wanted to talk about and she bit her lip to suppress her smile.

'Judging isn't helpful when we're trying to build a reputation as a liberal birthing unit. Obviously home birth isn't for everyone, but in this case, prior to the sudden foetal distress, her midwife had a healthy mother with good antenatal care and a history of a previous normal vaginal delivery. That's low risk.' She slanted a look at him and saw that his eyes were glazing. She'd have one more go.

'Do you realise that human beings are the only animals who make a nice safe nest to live in then leave it to have their young in a strange place? Don't you find that bizarre?'

'Bizarre? No.' That was too much for him.

Poppy got the feeling she'd suddenly grown another head.

He shook his head in disbelief. 'To come to a hospital to have your child seems perfectly natural to me—and something any sensible person would do.' His forehead creased.

'Look, I came back to check on the baby and I don't know why I offered to walk you to your bike.

Though it's probably because I don't like to see women walking alone at night.'

'Oh, I appreciate that.' She had no doubt he was wishing he hadn't, and Poppy tried hard not to let the amusement come through into her voice. She needn't have worried. He still couldn't come to terms with women wanting home births.

'What about infant mortality and morbidity? These people are dangerous.' He looked down at her walking beside him. 'No,' he said again. 'I don't find it bizarre and we'll never agree on home births.' He smiled to soften the words but his voice was harsh.

Poppy shrugged. 'Maybe we could talk about it another day?'

'I don't think so.'

They both stopped beside her red scooter. He stared at the tiny vehicle and its bottletop-sized wheels.

'What an embarrassing bike.'

Poppy laughed out loud. And she'd been worried about offending him? 'Oh very diplomatic, Dr Sheppard. I bet what you drive doesn't cost less than a soft drink to run every month, and it's fun. Have you heard of fun?'

He obviously wasn't used to being paid back and she smiled as he blinked at her tone.

'I'm sorry, that was rude of me,' he said. 'Which reminds me, I left rather quickly without telling you how impressed I was with your resuscitation skills. I thought we worked well together.'

Damn. She'd just decided he was an insufferable

prig and he said something nice. She hated that. Now she felt like a louse.

She tried to hide her face by bending down to put the keys in the ignition. She could feel the heat in her cheeks because he'd made her feel self-conscious with his comment.

'Thank you, Dr Sheppard.'

'Jake, please.'

'Jake, then. You're pretty good yourself at what you do. I'm Poppy.'

He raised his eyebrows.

Poppy sighed. 'My mother was a sixties flower child and she named her daughters after her favourite flowers. My sister's name is Jasmine.'

Jake glanced down at her. She was tall for a woman and well rounded. He liked the way her red hair curled and bounced around her face. It was a big improvement on the theatre cap. She looked like a poppy. She had one of those husky, sexy voices that seemed to come out of the most unlikely people.

He watched her face soften when she spoke of her mother, and it made him think of the way she'd looked at the baby outside Theatre. Her face wasn't beautiful—except when she smiled. Yet she had the kind of face he could watch all day, waiting for the changes. He couldn't remember the last time he'd enjoyed watching a woman's reactions so much.

Then she smiled and he realised that had been what he'd been waiting for. She lit up from within and the power of it scrambled his brains again. She could light a dark room with that smile. It made him catch his breath. Like the moment in Theatre when the baby had first cried. He was probably hypoglycaemic. Light-headedness and low blood sugar levels had a lot to answer for. He needed to get away from her.

'Well, Poppy, you should be safe if I leave you now.' He went to shake her hand but stopped at the expression on her face. He couldn't believe it. She looked like she was trying not to laugh. At him. He glared at her. She bit her lip and took the hand he'd let fall. She held it in both of hers and shook it.

'I'm sorry. Not that I don't appreciate the thought or your combat skills, Jake, but this is Midcoast.' She gestured around at the deserted street. 'Not Sydney or New York.'

The ungrateful minx.

'You're laughing at me.' He couldn't remember the last time someone hadn't taken him seriously. Then there had been that crack about fun. He froze. That was a worry. What was he turning into? Then she smiled that smile again.

'I'm sure you'll recover.'

She was playing the cheeky minx again, but she intrigued him. Still, he knew better than to lose his usual common sense. He'd always said that women in the health profession didn't attract him. Women required more than he could give. Look at his marriage before Helen had died.

He was here to do the work he loved. His eyes narrowed. And make someone, somewhere in this small country town pay for his brother's death, he reminded himself. He couldn't forget why he'd come here—to find the woman responsible for stealing a month of his brother's short life.

Someone had to fight against the new wave of

alternative remedies that were causing people to turn their backs on real medicine. Maybe she was one of them.

The herbal scent in Poppy's hair drifted to him and he found himself staring at her. One part of him sneered at her irresponsible stand on home births and the other half was sliding into a whirlpool of attraction that he knew was dangerous. But for the first time in nearly three years he felt alive. Something had shifted or cracked to allow some light in. He didn't know if it felt good or not, but it was hard to back away.

If he ignored the voice of reason he had listened to for years, he could just cup her chin in his hand and drop a swift kiss on her parted lips. Just one.

Jake stepped back. She encouraged people to condemn conventional medical care. Just like the woman who'd killed his brother. Hell, that had been close. He turned away. 'Goodnight, Sister.'

Poppy raised her eyebrows at the coldness and revulsion in his voice. The guy was all over the place. 'Goodnight, Jake! Nice meeting you, too.' She pulled her helmet on and puttered away as fast as the little bike could go.

CHAPTER TWO

POPPY felt unsettled all the way home. OK, so Jake was gorgeous. It might be amusing to bait him but it could be dangerous. Stop thinking with your hormones and think of the unit, she urged herself. She'd been crazy to risk alienating him by pushing home birth at him straight off, and then she'd laughed at him. He hadn't liked that. She giggled and bit her lip. It wasn't funny. But he was such a stuffed shirt.

It was a shame that what he stuffed in his shirt seemed to start a slow burn in her. Just when she'd thought her libido had been terminally extinguished. And doctors were definitely off the menu.

The next afternoon, Poppy arrived on the ward to start her shift. She barely had time to put her bag down before being hailed from the birthing room to assist.

Jake was the first person she saw as she entered the room and she instinctively bit back her smile. Strange how there still seemed to be time to notice how broad his shoulders looked in an open-necked white shirt that seemed to go on for ever across his chest. It wasn't fair that he affected her like this. Her life was fine without a man to complicate it. She frowned and pushed the thoughts away. She'd been through this last night and had decided not to be attracted to him.

Her glance flicked away to rest on the young girl in the final stages of labour. All seemed to be well in hand but she ensured that Dr Gates and the two morning midwives had everything needed before she moved over to the infant resuscitation trolley and Jake.

The paediatrician's presence meant that something wasn't right.

She raised her eyebrows in a silent question and he leaned over to speak softly in her ear.

'Lana is a sixteen-year-old first-time mum, due in ten weeks. She only came in half an hour ago and there was no time to send her off to the base hospital. She had a small antepartum haemorrhage at home and sudden onset of labour. No foetal heart rate found since admission.'

Poppy felt her stomach plummet. 'It still could have a chance.' Every midwife's worst nightmare was a mother left without a baby to take home.

'I haven't given up.' Jake's quiet words reinforced her sense of denial. She never gave up until the end. They had that much in common. When he continued with, 'NETS is on standby if the baby looks like it's going to make it.' He proved he was prepared to give the baby every chance.

The neonatal evacuation team from Newcastle Hospital flew to country areas with their own portable intensive-care unit, complete with highly trained nursing staff, all equipment and a neonatologist on board to stabilise the baby before transfer.

'I'll check the nursery crib.' She slipped out of the room to turn on the oxygen in the nursery humidicrib, then rolled two hot bunny rugs to lay over the trolley just prior to the baby being born.

When she returned to the unit she could see the tip of the baby's head as it descended down the birth canal. She arranged the blankets and Jake moved over to stand beside Dr Gates.

'If we can get a decent heart rate and keep the baby well oxygenated without doing any damage, it has a chance.'

More of the baby's head showed with each contraction until the tiny flaccid body eased gently into Dr Gates's large palm.

Poppy winced at the obvious signs of prematurity. Wrinkled, almost transparent skin covered in downy hair. Vernix, the white creamy substance that acted as a barrier cream in the womb, covered her body and the head seemed much larger than the body.

Quickly, Dr Gates clamped and cut the cord to enable Jake to whisk the baby over to the resuscitation trolley.

The ease and speed with which Jake assessed, suctioned, intubated and initiated CPR on the infant was something Poppy had to admire. As she watched those large hands giving cardiac massage to the tiny chest to encourage the little heart to beat, she found herself willing the baby to live. Her mouth was dry as she concentrated on being able to anticipate Jake's requests.

Barely a word passed between them in that fraught ten minutes. Her throat tightened as she saw the tiny hand clench and unclench as the baby's heart rate settled into a stable rhythm.

'Get NETS on the phone and on their way.' Jake's

quiet voice carried clearly to everyone in the room and Poppy blinked the mist from her eyes. She bit her lip and motioned to one of the morning midwives to do as he'd bidden.

'OK, Poppy, let's get her in the crib and I'll bag her until we can get her hooked up to the ventilator.' He looked up and gave the exhausted mum a quick grin. 'Congratulations, Lana, she's a beautiful girl. Bag for a second, please, Poppy.'

He swiftly swapped places with Poppy and she rhythmically squeezed the oxygen into the tiny lungs. Jake steered the awkward trolley against the bed and lifted Lana's hand to touch it to her baby's cheek. He raised his own to rest it reassuringly on the mother's head and said softly but firmly, 'Baby's going to have the best care we can give her, and she's a fighter.'

To take the time to reassure the child's mother made Jake a special man. Poppy had to admit it. A lot of doctors, including her ex-husband, were so one-tracked they didn't realise how much of a difference that one touch could make—to give a frightened parent that tiny second of hand contact with their child and create bonds and memories that couldn't be replaced with a Polaroid picture.

Only then did he allow them to wheel the trolley with its precious burden into the nursery. Away from her mother.

'The next hour will be a battle while we try to maintain the baby in as stable a condition as we can while we wait for the NETS team to arrive.'

They'd connected the baby to the electric ventilator, and the sound of the rhythmic breathing of the machine seemed to dominate the room. Jake's voice was low as he found a tiny vein into which to insert the even smaller cannula. Poppy could hardly see the blueness under the skin that showed him where to aim, but he slid it in with ease as she held baby's arm still.

'That's impressive. I have trouble finding a vein in mothers sometimes. Remind me not to complain again when I have those big veins to work with.'

He looked at her under his brows and half smiled. 'I've had lots of practice.'

By the time they had a drip running and the baby fully monitored, they could hear the thump of the helicopter.

Even though she'd seen it all before, it always amazed Poppy how much equipment a helicopter could disgorge when it arrived.

The specialist seemed to be surprised and pleased to see Jake, and even the flight sister was on a first-name basis with him.

Poppy turned away and pulled a face at herself for feeling superfluous. Surprised, she realised she felt vaguely annoyed with Jake and his easy camaraderie with the flight crew. She retreated to the birthing unit to take over from the morning midwife. Lana was tidying herself, preparing to go in the helicopter with her baby.

Soon the thump of the helicopter rotor faded into the distance and Poppy finished restocking the emergency trolley in case it was needed for the next delivery. She slowed her hands as she went over her feelings. All her nerve endings seemed to stand up and wave around whenever Jake was near her. She didn't even know the guy. Get a grip, girl, she told herself firmly.

Poppy heard Jake being paged for the children's ward, and breathed a sigh of relief. Then, just when she thought she was safe, he poked his head into the room.

'Poppy.'

His sudden voice made her jump and she spun around. She could hear her heart pounding in her ears and the room seemed suddenly airless. It was just that he'd startled her.

'Yes, Doctor?' Her voice sounded remarkably cool and she managed to meet his eyes. The more she saw of him the more jangled she became. It was really starting to be a pain.

'I'll drop back later—there's something I want to discuss with you.' His head disappeared around the door again.

Poppy leaned shakily back against the bench and let out a ragged breath. What was it with this man? She hugged her stomach. How could he reduce her to this?

She'd make herself a remedy when she finished tonight. An essential oil bath perhaps, with a calming and stabilising blend for her nerves out of Mum's aromatherapy book.

It should help.

As usual, thinking of her radical, lovable mother lifted her spirits. Although it had only been two years since she'd died, Poppy had taken to heart her mother's conviction that in spirit she would always be with her, and the ache of loss was bearable.

Maybe Poppy had compensated by immersing

herself in her mother's interests, like aromatherapy and reflexology, and her home was certainly filled with her mother's beads, plants and chimes. But they fitted so beautifully into midwifery, and just maybe, she admitted wryly, anything that attracted her ex-husband's contempt had become doubly attractive to Poppy. The guy was a weasel and hated anything unconventional.

She wondered if Jake did, then shook her head. It didn't matter anyway. She wasn't going to get close enough to find out.

Sandy should be around here somewhere, she thought, and found her friend helping the new mums to master the art of breastfeeding. She was in Sheila's room. Sheila's eyes showed their delight when she saw Poppy.

'How are you today, Sheila? Not too tired, I hope?' Poppy noted the rings around the girl's eyes but her contentment with her new son was plain to see. 'Not quite the natural birth you and Luke were planning, was it? Though, I must admit, you do make beautiful babies.'

Sheila smiled dreamily at her son. 'I'm feeling much better this afternoon, but thanks, Poppy, for looking after us yesterday. You were wonderful. I was so scared of coming into the hospital and how I'd be treated—let alone having a Caesarean. Luke was here when Dr Sheppard came in to see me this morning, and he's very impressed with him.' She winked. 'Dr Sheppard's quite a hunk.'

'Yes, he is.' Poppy felt her face stiffen at the mention of Jake and changed the subject. 'You and Cade look very contented there. I'll come back later to see you. Sandy and I are going to have a much-needed cuppa. If you want us, just push the buzzer.'

The two women moved towards the tea room and Poppy grimaced as she saw Sandy watching her. For the last two years her friend had been trying to encourage her to date. Without much success.

'So, do you think the "hunky" Dr Sheppard is going to fit in here, Poppy? You're the one who's had the most to do with him. Day staff said he calls you by your first name already.' Sandy's eyes glinted mischievously.

Poppy avoided her eyes. 'He's certainly good-looking, but I learnt long ago what that means. At least he's good at his job.'

'Good-looking? The guy is devastating. I fancy him myself and I'm ten years too old for him and happily married. You haven't even hit thirty. Come on, Poppy, when are you going to give another man a chance?'

'That's just it, Sandy. Why should I? I dumped my inferiority complexes with my married name. My life is great. Why would I risk that again?'

Maybe she shouldn't visit the sins of her ex-husband on Jake. Maybe he was trustworthy.

Ha! That small voice inside her went into hysterics. You've met him twice! The guy's charming, but can he be trusted?

'When Mum died, another "hunk" walked out on me, right when I needed him. Maybe I'd feel more inclined to trust him if he wasn't so perfect.'

Sandy raised her eyebrows. 'Yeah, right. So we need him to put a paper bag over his head and get him to chant, ''Trust me, trust me.''' Poppy stifled a giggle at her friend's imagination.

As if conjured up by their conversation, the sound of slightly off-key whistling preceded Jake's head as he appeared around the door. Poppy watched his eyes brighten at seeing them and his long lean body followed to prop up the door frame. His dark hair was tousled as if he'd been caught in a wild breeze and the front of his shirt was damp and sticking to him in a fist-sized spot under his collarbone.

Jake looked a different man from the one in the nursery today. Ten years seemed to have dropped off his age. 'I love kids, even if they are messy. I like the way they run Children's Ward here—*for* the kids and not *despite* them.' He grinned at them.

Poppy could see he meant what he said. She felt the same about her own ward.

'Coffee smells good.' Jake's voice slid through her defences and Poppy stiffened her shoulders. Sandy could be mother.

'How do you like it, Dr Sheppard?' Sandy switched on the jug.

'Jake, please. I'd settle for any way, except down the front of my shirt like my last drink was given to me. I can see by your badge that you're Sandy. Is it Sandra or Cassandra?'

'Cassandra, actually.' Sandy blushed and Poppy hid her smile as the mature mother of three groped for composure like a sixteen-year-old.

'White, no sugar, thanks.'

Cynically, Poppy marvelled at the way Jake put Sandy at her ease, drawing the older woman out about her children, obviously interested in all she said. Handsome men usually could. She could remember her ex-husband and all the young mothers sighing over him. Her nose twitched in disgust.

'I'm going to check the ward.' Poppy stood abruptly and left the room as if she had something important to do. She didn't. She heard his voice thanking Sandy for the coffee as she walked away and she knew he'd follow her. She sighed.

The corridor was deserted and as Poppy passed one of the empty rooms she felt his presence as he came up behind her and steered her into it with a hand on her shoulder. He gently shut the door behind them.

Poppy could hear the now familiar thumping in her ears and she tried to slow the rapid rise and fall of her breathing as she turned to face him. She tried for lightness. 'Did you want to see me, Doctor?'

Jake's face was calm and Poppy marvelled how difficult she found it to read his mood. He was different again from the man of ten minutes ago. He didn't look like he was going to chastise her for some fault in her work or even discuss a patient—so why was he here?

'I want to apologise—for last night. There are reasons, which have nothing to do with you, that may have made me seem unfriendly.'

'Apology accepted, Dr Sheppard.' She looked up at him with mischief in her eyes. 'Be polite next time.'

'My mother would like you, Poppy. She's very proper, too.' He grinned and held out his hand for her to shake.

'Proper' was such an old-fashioned word. Poppy

hiccuped on a giggle as she thought of herself as being labelled proper. But she supposed he'd only seen her as a neonatal nurse.

Actually, there had been times she'd been labelled a hippie, and a harpy—'like your mother'. Her husband's cold contempt still stung after all this time.

She was sure conservative Mrs Sheppard wouldn't appreciate Poppy's views or her mother's past. Poppy couldn't exactly tell Jake that.

'Thank you,' she said politely.

'To friendship, as long as you don't try to convince me that having a home birth is a responsible choice for a parent.'

He smiled at her but she could see he really meant what he'd said. She wondered what he'd think about her complementary therapies in the birthing unit. She shrugged. He'd find out.

He added, 'I have asked you to call me Jake, please.'

'To friendship, then, Jake.' She reached out and placed her hand in his, and the difference in hand size made her feel suddenly very feminine. 'But don't expect me not to try and change your mind.' Sensation tingled up her arm. She bit her lip. Friendship with this man would be…difficult!

By nine o'clock that night everything was quiet on the ward. Poppy was sitting with Sandy, writing patient reports, when the internal paging system suddenly erupted with noise. The medical emergency buzzer. This drew at least one staff member from each ward to assist in the area illuminated on the board.

'I'll go, Sandy.' Poppy jogged quickly down the corridor and her stomach tightened as she saw the initials of the ward involved. Children's Ward. Maternity was the closest unit and Poppy skidded around the corner and through the door. Like Maternity, Children's Ward was staffed by only two nurses a shift. They'd need help. She scanned the indicators for the room with the light on and drew a quick breath as she entered.

She could see the child's eyes were huge and terrified in her pale face. The sister in charge of the ward was supporting the girl and speaking gently, trying to reassure her. The hiss of the oxygen blowing the Ventolin mist into the girl's lungs dominated the room as the child tried to force her narrowed bronchial tubes to open enough to let the air in.

'Poppy! Thank God.' The sister in charge looked up briefly. 'Amelia was admitted this evening with her asthma, and she's not responding to the Ventolin this time.'

The junior nurse wheeled the emergency trolley into the room and looked as frightened as the patient.

'Have you rung Dr Sheppard?' Poppy could see the little girl becoming more and more sleepy as she tried to lean forward droopily on her thin arms. She felt her nerves tighten as she remembered the words of her intensive care tutor. A sleepy asthmatic is an asthmatic in trouble.

'Haven't had time, but Nurse can ring now that you're here to stay with me.' The junior hurried to the door. 'Tell him urgently, please.'

'I'll do the trolley part. She knows you. You keep her as calm as possible. Where are her parents?'

'Her father's gone home to feed the animals. You've got her mother over in Maternity.' Poppy checked the girl's armband and realised that this was Sheila's older child. Heck!

'She hasn't an intravenous line *in situ*?'

'It leaked into the tissues an hour ago and I paged the resident to resite it, but he's stuck in Casualty with a chest-pain case. Dr Sheppard's going to kill me because I didn't ring him to come back.'

Poppy winced. He probably would, but that was the least of their problems at the moment. 'I'll have to cannulate if Jake doesn't get here soon. How old is she? I need to work out the dosage for the drug.' She hoped she wouldn't mess up any veins but it was no use worrying—she had to do it. They'd need adrenalin if the child became much worse. Amelia started to cough, with the bronchospasm in her air passages making the air entry even more difficult.

'She's six.'

Poppy drew up the adrenalin and taped the ampoule to the syringe. It was situations like these that the wrong drugs could be accidentally given if they weren't easily identified. She laid it in an injection tray and assembled the equipment to set up the IV.

Come on, Jake. She knew she was being unreasonable to expect him to appear as soon as he was called. It had probably been only a couple of minutes since the buzzer had gone off. Staff from other wards were arriving and the room seemed crowded with people. Unfortunately, most of them didn't know what to do.

Poppy could see that the little girl was getting very little air in now and her chest was barely moving. A moment of panic welled up at the thought of her dying, but Poppy squashed it down.

'She needs IPPV with the mask.'

'I've got it here.' One of the sisters from Intensive Care arrived and moved to commence intermittent positive pressure to force the lungs to open for the Ventolin and oxygen.

'Someone grab the automatic blood-pressure machine and we need to know her oxygen saturation, too. Someone else get a clipboard and write down the times and any drugs given.' Poppy's voice was controlled and quiet but the response was immediate.

She placed a tourniquet on the child's arm. She couldn't even see any veins to aim for as the lack of oxygen had shut down the peripheral circulation to keep as much blood flow to the brain as possible. If she gave the injection into the muscle it could take several vital minutes for it to be picked up and dispersed by the blood to take effect and allow the bronchioles to dilate.

It would have to be intravenous! The thought of Jake's ability to find the baby's vein earlier that day strengthened her, and she slid the needle into the largest vein in the bend of Amelia's arm. The immediate back-flow of blood made her heave a quick sigh of relief as she taped it into position.

'Not the best place for one but good in an emergency.' Jake's voice behind her left shoulder made Poppy sigh in relief. 'What happened to the other one?'

'It tissued!' Poppy turned and moved aside for Jake to get to the little girl.

Jake's voice was quietly reassuring. 'Amelia, it's Dr Sheppard. You'll be OK. Sweetheart, just try and relax.' He held his hand out behind him and Poppy placed the tray in his hand. 'Adrenalin?' He checked the ampoule and fitted the syringe onto the intravenous port then slowly squeezed in the drug. 'How much would you have given, Poppy?'

'Age times two plus eight. About two mils over three minutes, but I haven't checked it with anyone yet.'

Jake glanced up at her briefly and nodded. 'Pretty good for a woman who deals with babies.'

He turned back to the little girl. 'This should ease your breathing in a minute or so, Amelia. Hang in there.'

The girl was barely conscious and the sound of the rhythmic squeezing of air into Amelia's lungs punctuated the rapid beeping of the monitors connected to the child. She looked worse, if anything, and Poppy was starting to feel cold with dread.

Jake's face was stone-like, as if he was willing the child to improve, but they both knew that children responded better than adults did to the treatment—if it was received in time.

The next minute dragged. Jake said, 'Come on, Amelia. Try and cough, sweetheart.' The girl's eyelids fluttered and then opened wide in fear. She gave a tiny huff of expelled air and then started to cough. Over the next few minutes her colour improved as she rid herself of some of the extra secretions blocking her lungs.

Poppy sagged against the wall. The crisis was over. Amelia was still a sick little girl and would be transferred to the intensive care unit for careful monitoring, but the immediate danger was over. Poppy met the eyes of the children's ward sister in relief.

The other woman mouthed her thanks as Poppy hand-signalled that she was leaving. Suddenly she had to get out of there. Poppy knew it was just a delayed reaction to the stress, but the full horror of how close Amelia had come to dying crashed in on her. Jake would go and see Sheila as soon as he could safely leave her daughter's side. It had been a big day all round and she decided she needed some space to pull her thoughts together.

Sandy was waiting for her when she came back. 'Poppy? You look like you've seen a ghost. What happened?'

'I'm OK. Everything will be all right now. There was a six-year-old with a severe asthma attack. Sheila's daughter.'

Sandy drew her breath in sharply.

Poppy looked up at her friend. 'Yeah, it was touch and go for a while there before Jake arrived. I had to cannulate.' She looked at her hands, saw they were shaking and tucked them behind her back. 'I'd rather have a problem in labour any day.'

Sandy reached into her pocket. 'Time out, friend. Have a butterscotch.' Poppy gave her a watery grin and took the sweet.

'Thanks. I need a cup of tea, too. How's the ward?'

By the time they were ready to go home, Poppy had stopped running the scene over in her mind to see if she should have done something differently. As she walked towards her bike she could see a figure that was becoming familiar standing outside the entrance to Casualty. She veered towards him.

'Jake?' What are you doing out here?'

He looked up, but his smile didn't reach his eyes. 'Getting some air before I go over and see Amelia's mother.'

Poppy felt the fear in her throat and forced the words out. 'Amelia's all right, isn't she?'

'She will be. Rest and Ventolin for the next couple of days should improve her.' His gaze held hers. 'You did a terrific job, Poppy. If I'd had to wait another few minutes, putting in the cannula, we may not have been so lucky.' He hit one fist into his other hand. 'People don't realise how dangerous asthma is!'

His tone was forceful with disgust and Poppy couldn't help thinking of the poor sister who hadn't told him about resiting the cannula. She had a feeling the sister had copped it. But everyone was human and Poppy felt sorry for her. She sighed.

'I'm tired. See you, Jake.' She turned to go and she caught his movement as he pushed himself off the wall to follow her.

'I'll walk you to your bike.'

Poppy slanted a look up at him. 'This is getting to be a habit.'

'I've never liked a woman walking alone at night. It's not safe. She should have a man to protect her.'

Poppy couldn't help the bubble of laughter that slipped out. 'Oh, spare me. I live on my own and walk myself to my bike every time I'm working late. Nothing's ever happened to me and never will.'

A car passed and she saw the lift of one eyebrow at her comment. 'My hero,' she murmured facetiously under her breath, and smiled in the dark as she stopped beside her bike.

'I heard that.' He put his hand on her arm and pulled her to face him. 'I could kiss you if I wanted to and you wouldn't be able to stop me.'

She looked up at him and gave another gurgle of laughter. 'Or I could kiss you and you wouldn't know what hit you.' She tilted her head and smiled at him. He was so old-fashioned. 'Goodnight, Jake.'

Poppy parked her scooter under the carport and sat for a moment with her helmet off. She could feel her smile. Poppy knew she was playing with fire but it had been so long since she'd felt that sort of reaction to a man. It must be too long because she couldn't remember it. Even with Tyson. She shook her head to get rid of the thought.

Men could turn their emotion on and off like a tap. Why couldn't women? There'd been undercurrents there she couldn't help noticing. Her heart felt like a burst water main.

She wasn't going to become involved with a doctor. Especially not with another one who felt threatened by the true meaning of midwifery. Once had been enough. It had been the topic of the day when Dr Tyson Harvey had left his wife to run off with a consultant's daughter.

Her first husband had been a smooth talker and too handsome. Just like this guy. When Tyson had wanted something, he'd gazed into her eyes and switched on his charm until she'd bent to his will. She'd tried to transform herself into the type of wife he'd wanted, but she'd always seemed to fail him. She hadn't even realised she'd failed herself—until he'd left.

Poppy cringed. She wouldn't set herself up like that again. Ever.

CHAPTER THREE

THE birthing unit was dimly lit and peaceful. The scent of lavender wafted lightly past Poppy from the aromatherapy vaporiser as she unhurriedly attended to the last-minute tasks before the baby's birth. Soft rain-forest noises tinkled in the corner of the room from the CD player.

'The bath water's ready, Phillip.' Poppy's voice barely rose above the music as she dried her hands on a towel.

Followers of a Leboyer birth believed that the newborn benefited greatly from the return to weightlessness in the bath soon after delivery to allow a more gentle transition into the world. They believed this practice encouraged babies to be less stressed and more settled both in the immediate days following birth and in later life.

Poppy liked the idea but preferred no loss of contact from the mother once the child was born, usually leaving baby and mother skin to skin for at least an hour. It was her job to meet the needs of the parents to ensure they achieved as positive a birth experience as possible. As long as it was safe. If they wanted bath water, they got bath water.

Phillip, the father of the child, was stripped to the waist and lovingly held his wife's shoulders as she bore down strongly with the contraction.

Poppy could see that Carolyn, the woman giving

birth, was fiercely concentrating. She sat up with her arms under her thighs; the large blue beanbag supported her as she strained to see the child's head reflected in the mirror at the end of the bed.

'I can see it. Look. Black hair.' Carolyn puffed.

Phillip and Poppy smiled at each other as Carolyn seemed to gain strength from the sight of her child easing its way down the birth canal.

Poppy savoured the aura of tranquillity they had created for the new arrival. This was midwifery at its least intrusive. If only the medical profession could have felt the ambience in the room she would have converted the lot of them.

Poppy heard a gentle knock and Jake's head appeared around the door. She looked up and beckoned him in. This was in the safety of a hospital. Not a home. Surely he would see that non-intervention could be good and then he could help her convince the sceptics left in the hospital.

She fingered the peace sign around her neck. It gave her a thrill to see him. She hadn't seen him for a week and he'd intruded on her thoughts more than she liked. It seemed as if her colleagues continually sang his praises. She smiled a welcome.

Unnoticed by the parents, Jake slipped to Poppy's side and nodded. Disappointment hit her like a stone when, instead of appreciation for the setting, an almost bitter grimace crossed his face.

She watched him sniff and glance around the room, his eyebrows rising at the sight of a chunk of rose quartz the size of a small shoebox resting on the bedside table. He glared at the reflexology chart discarded on another table, before he schooled his features to impassiveness.

He whispered into her ear, 'Dr Gates received your message but he's been held up in Theatre. He should be along shortly and I said I'd pass the message along.'

He turned to go. 'By the way, Sister, I hope there's no naked flame burning that oil in case you have to turn the oxygen on. Surely you're aware of that?'

Poppy frowned at his tone. His voice had remained quiet but had vibrated with a deep anger that seemed totally out of place. What had she done? It was almost as if he could hardly bear to speak to her.

'Thank you, Doctor,' she answered evenly, her own voice soft and not carrying to the others in the room. 'I always use an electric aromatherapy vaporiser. Of course I'm aware of the danger of hospital oxygen and naked flames.' She tilted her head. 'There's no indication that this child will require oxygen, Jake.'

He nodded curtly, gave one final look of revulsion around the room and then was gone.

A chill ran over her neck and Poppy shivered. She hated that. People with negative feelings should be nowhere near a birthing room. She glared at the shut door and shook off the feeling of disquiet to concentrate once again on the magical tableau before her. She wouldn't allow him to ruin the mood.

Everything proceeded smoothly and Poppy stood back as Carolyn controlled the birth of the baby's head by her own gentle efforts. Phillip cut the cord when it stopped pulsating and the bath scene made Poppy think of Christmas and mangers and what she was missing in her own life.

It was at times like these that she mourned the death of her dreams. She'd assumed when she'd married Tyson that this would have been a scene from their lives together. She couldn't have been more wrong.

Still, maybe one day, a long time in the future, if she found a man she could trust not to try and stamp out all the things that were important to her, a baby would be hers. For the moment she gained great personal joy from helping other parents to achieve their dreams of a tranquil and natural birth.

Ironically, it wasn't until her own husband had departed that this type of birth had become accepted at Midcoast.

Poppy helped settle the baby at her mother's breast then left the new family alone together. She sighed as she shut the door quietly behind her.

An hour later, she stood in the shower at home, washing away the tensions of the shift as she went over her day. The new baby girl had been pink and placid, and not one cry had passed her rosebud lips, much to Poppy's satisfaction. Phillip and Carolyn were ecstatic and would probably take their new daughter home that afternoon.

Yet she felt drained. It wasn't like her to feel this way. It must be the responsibility of ensuring that all went well, she decided. Sometimes it weighed her down but the pleasure and satisfaction of a job well done was worth it. So why wasn't she euphoric? She stepped out and towelled herself thoughtfully.

The chimes connected to the doorbell tinkled noisily. 'Hang on.' They'd have to wait. She pulled on her undies, slipped her batik caftan over her head and combed her wet hair. Only then did she answer the door.

It was Jake. She tilted her head. How had he known where she lived? His face was set in uncompromising lines and his greeting was abrupt, as if he had a lot on his mind. 'May I come in?'

By the look on his face she didn't know whether it was a good idea or not. But, then, who was she kidding? She couldn't have made herself turn him away. 'I suppose so, Jake. Come through.' She gestured with her hand as she fought down the agitation his presence created in her stomach.

She had to admit that a lot of the time he just plain overwhelmed her. Hopefully her expression was as calm as she wanted to look. She'd only met him a few times but each time he seemed to be a different person. Maybe he had twelve personalities. Like Sibyl, that woman in the movie. She bit her lip to stop a smile.

He hesitated at the door so she went first, but he didn't follow her. She turned back to see what he was doing. What *was* he doing? She didn't need this.

'I didn't invite you here, Jake. If you don't want to come in, why are you here?'

Poppy stood with her hands on her hips and waited for his eyes to meet hers. She watched him run his hands through his hair, a gesture that made him seem vulnerable. Something was bothering him seriously, and she softened towards him again.

He said, 'I asked Sandy where you lived.'

When he finally moved into the house, she found it intriguing the way his head turned to note the abundant plant life, colourful mobiles and wind chimes and obviously Indian influence, so popular in the sixties, that dominated her house. He compressed his lips and nodded his head. 'I should have known.'

'Should have known what, Jake?' Poppy tapped her foot, which wasn't like her.

'You're one of those ''alternative'' people aren't you, Poppy?'

She squared her shoulders and stared up at him as she weighed up the best way to present her argument. He topped her height by a good six inches and she had the feeling that every inch might count.

'What's your definition of ''alternative'', Jake?' She held his eyes. 'Are we talking Greenie? Hippy?' Her hands were back on her hips. 'Maybe dangerous radical?' She raised her eyebrows. 'Or just someone who believes in something you don't understand?'

He blinked at her tone. Tough, she thought. If he wants a lecture he's come to the right place. Poppy read the surprise on his face and felt the familiar zeal to share her passion for complementary therapies.

'Come on, Jake. I saw your face in the birthing unit—your reactions to the piece of quartz soaking up the negative vibes, the twitch of your nose and curl of your lip at the scent of aromatherapy and the bath.' She spun on her heel and walked a couple of paces away, before turning back to face him. 'I believe in holistic midwifery—which is the use of *all* techniques that can help the clients. What's your problem with that?'

They glared at each other and she watched his eyes narrow.

'Hocus-pocus, Poppy. Natural doesn't automatically mean safe. There is no scientific proof that these methods work. No controlled studies have been done. I have a problem with people leaning on other "techniques" as you call them—and I think they're dangerous. When something goes wrong it's my *conventional* medicine...' he tapped his chest with a finger '...that's going to save them—if they can be saved and haven't been too messed up by quacks trying to create miracles with a piece of rock.'

He snorted. 'The lights were so dim, how could you see whether the baby was a good colour? What was the baby's temperature when you'd finished dipping it in and out of the bloody Leboyer bath?'

By the time he'd finished his tirade his voice had risen. She blinked then stared at him hard. This man was hurting. Goose-bumps lifted the hairs on her arms. The feeling that something wasn't right assumed enormous proportions.

She took a deep breath. 'I'm not deaf, Jake. On the surface, your arguments are old school and nothing I can't demolish.' Once her husband had left, it had taken her two years to knock the snickers out of medical and nursing staff at her 'holistic' deliveries.

'But there's something deeper and more personal

in this explosion of emotion. What experiences have you had with alternative therapies, Jake?' She gentled her voice. She didn't want to cause him pain. Wasn't even sure of the reaction she might get, let alone the fallout—but it was too late.

'I'll tell you!' The three words were made more chilling by the softness in his voice.

She stared, mesmerised, into his ice-blue eyes. She felt he was looking right through her into the past. The sense of foreboding settled over her like a hail-filled cloud and she sucked her breath in with the premonition that this was going to hurt her as much as him.

He went on in that strange, quiet voice, as if it wasn't necessary now to add volume to the emotion in it.

'I've seen people waste away until they were pale, skeletal shadows of themselves. Too late to help, yet if they'd agreed sooner they might have been saved—all in the name of holistic medicine.'

The pace of his words increased as if he had to say it quickly or he wouldn't be able to finish. He drew a breath. 'These quacks have no idea of the damage they cause and I'd outlaw them if I could.'

She ached to smooth the lines of strain from his face and his anger vibrated so thickly that Poppy was amazed her wind chimes weren't ringing.

Jake's eyes seem to refocus on her face, and softened marginally. 'I really hate the way people can be brainwashed by the disadvantages of conventional medicine, often to such a degree that they choose alternative medicines as the "best" treatment. I've seen tragedies which I believe, could have been prevented.'

This was dangerous ground and Poppy could see the edges of his self-control fraying as he spoke.

'Who was it, Jake?'

At first she thought he hadn't heard her words and she followed the play of emotions across his strong face. She saw the vulnerability he tried so hard to conceal. Then suddenly the vulnerability was gone as if it had never been, and the anger inside him etched harsh lines down the sides of his mouth. The shutter fell across his face like a window shutting out the storm.

'My brother. He died of cancer in the hands of a herbalist.'

The stark words echoed around the room until they seemed to sink into the polished floorboards in front of her feet, lying there between her and him, dormant, waiting to strike again.

Poppy's throat tightened as she saw his distress. The strength of her desire to pull his head down on her breast and soothe the lines from his face took her aback.

'Sit down.' She indicated the batik-covered lounge and he frowned as if unsure how he came to be there. He grimaced as he folded his long frame onto the low couch and then, as if surprised by its comfort, he leaned his head back against the headrest and closed his eyes for a moment.

She sank down beside his legs on the floor and took his hand. There was nothing sexual in it, just comfort from one human being to another.

'Can you tell me about it, Jake?'

He opened his eyes wearily. 'I will never forgive that woman.' The statement was flat and irrevocable. 'OK. So the surgery didn't get it all but he could have had more chemotherapy and radiotherapy. Damn it, I had the best specialists in the country ready to help him and he just disappeared one day. He didn't come home until it was too late.

'He'd been living with her and being treated—' he almost spat the word '—holistically.' I don't know her name. Just that she lived around here somewhere. Do you know what was so ironic, Poppy? He actually said I should see her myself as she could do a lot for me.' He laughed mirthlessly. 'I came here tonight thinking maybe you would know who she was.'

Poppy felt that dreadful shiver of premonition run down her spine again.

Surely fate wouldn't be so cruel. Not James! Her mother's last patient before she'd become sick herself. Poppy felt the nausea rise in her throat at the ramifications if that was true. Jake was staring into the distance and continued on, oblivious to Poppy's distress. She could see the resemblance again.

'It was nearly three years ago, but I'll never forgive that woman. He might still be living if she hadn't poisoned his mind against conventional medicine. I was his brother. Why couldn't he listen to what I was saying?'

Poppy swallowed the lump in her throat and drew such a deep breath into her lungs that it felt as if it reached her toes. She breathed out. 'Jake.' He turned towards her. 'Can you prove that was why he died? Was there really much chance of aggressive medical treatment curing him? What chances did your conventional specialists give him and what sort of hell would they have put him through?'

He pulled his hand from hers. 'I don't believe it. You sound like my mother.' His voice was laden with disgust. 'How do you think I felt, being a doctor and unable to save my own brother. I failed and I live with that every day. I'll find that woman and I'll make her sorry she ever met me. At the moment it looks as though my brother covered his and her tracks too well for her to be held accountable, but I'll find her. She poisoned him against me.'

Poppy let go of his hand and stared at him sternly. 'Are you sure you aren't the person who's been poisoned, Jake?' She tried another tack. 'What were you thinking when you came here tonight?'

'When I saw all the paraphernalia in that labour ward today it made my skin crawl! I look around this house and it's how I imagined that woman's house would look. And I admit that you attract me, despite myself. I guess I was hoping it wouldn't be like this. Or that you weren't a woman who believes in the very trappings I despise. I have to go.'

She winced at the pain his statement caused and some instinctive protection mode switched on and directed her tongue. 'I never asked you to be attracted to me, Jake. We barely know each other, and the last thing I want in my life is negative vibes from you.' Their eyes met and then both looked away.

He levered himself out of the couch. The room still echoed with the unleashed emotions of the last ten minutes. Maybe that was why they were so aware of each other.

'Goodbye, Jake.'

He stared into her eyes, as if trying to read the meaning beneath her simple words.

'Goodnight, Poppy.'

Poppy lay sleepless most of that night. Relaxation music, visualisation of a special place, even punching pillows couldn't rid her mind of the look of pain in Jake's eyes.

If she didn't totally believe that James had benefited from her mother's care, she wouldn't have been able to bear it.

She could clearly remember the first day she'd met James. He'd told her that he'd heard of Rose McCrae through a friend running a health-food shop. When he'd talked of finding somewhere calm and relaxing for a couple of weeks to get his head together, her mother's name had come up.

He'd moved in and had seemed to absorb the ambience of calm that surrounded Rose. Tall, like Jake, he'd had the same incredible blue eyes. But James had been thin, pale and stressed, and Poppy had known there had to be something terribly wrong.

Yet he'd never been negative or bitter about his illness. He'd chosen not to accept aggressive medical treatment which had promised short-term improvement in his condition. He'd kept in phone contact with his parents, but after the first two calls to his brother he'd admitted it had been too stressful dealing with Jake's anger.

He'd only stayed a month but the mental change in him had been wonderful. Despite the progression of his illness he'd been calm, peaceful and even wickedly humorous about his condition. Rose and Poppy had felt privileged to have spent the time with him, and Poppy believed that, indirectly, James had helped their acceptance of Rose's illness two months later.

Now she had to deal with Jake.

How did you tell a man that your own mother was his focus for three years of anger?

Poppy winced at the thought of Jake's suppressed bitterness falling on her head but then she shrugged.

He couldn't possibly say any worse things to her than the 'snake' had. She must have been more vulnerable then. Also, she'd been young and in love with her handsome husband. She smiled without humour as she remembered.

She could never figure out why Tyson had married her when he'd spent all of their marriage trying to ridicule her into conservatism. 'Don't wear bright colours—you look gaudy. Don't burn that hippy stuff in my house and take down those irritating chimes. Your mother is an embarrassment.' He hadn't been able to believe he'd been related to a woman who'd been arrested for participating in anti-Vietnam protests.

Looking back now, Poppy could almost laugh at how annoyed Tyson had been when he'd realised he'd married the wrong woman. He'd tried to steer her away from holistic midwifery, but after he'd left her she'd immersed herself in alternative therapies for childbirth until she'd unwittingly become the local expert—and she was proud of that.

Now, more than two years later, she found herself attracted to another man who abhorred the unconventional. This was definitely a good time to learn from her mistakes.

Tomorrow was Sunday. When she had the weekend off she usually took her nephews to the club day for junior lifesavers at the beach. She wouldn't have time to think about Jake.

She punched her pillow again.

Poppy's bed was a wreck by the time she woke the next morning. Exhausted, she felt rumpled, like an old paper bag. It had been a rush she hadn't needed to get the boys to Nippers on time.

Crescent Head Beach, usually a sleepy place, was busy on a Sunday morning. Poppy could see at least a dozen beach umbrellas. Through the week she'd have been lucky to see one. A bit different to the beaches in Sydney. She was late and herded the boys quickly across the beach, wincing at the sand's heat already stinging the soles of her feet.

A lifesaver's loudhailer boomed from behind. 'Would the lady with the blue hat please stop.'

Poppy slowed, and touched the hat on her head. She glanced back and shielded her eyes from the morning sun.

The tall lifesaver was pointing to her. He waved his hand with something in it. She stared harder and she realised she must have dropped her purse. 'Hell,' she muttered under her breath.

Her three nephews stopped a little ahead of her to see what was happening, and she shooed them onwards to the Nippers tent to be marked off the attendance roll.

As she retraced her steps to retrieve her purse she

could feel the weight of the man's appraisal lifting the fine hairs on her arms. Authority rested naturally on him, and it wasn't only his size. He was big. Familiarly big. Familiarly gorgeous. Under the hat…it was Jake. How embarrassing. He'd think she was scatterbrained as well as loopy. Her mind might have been embarrassed but she had to acknowledge that her body seemed glad to see him. Damn adrenalin again.

Since the divorce she hadn't trusted herself to be interested in the opposite sex, but there was something about this man that stirred excitement in the pit of her stomach, down her legs, between her toes…

It was a shame there was no future in it. They'd been through it last night and she didn't need to go there again. Damn it, his initials should stand for Sam Edger X-ray.

She tried to study him dispassionately as she walked towards him. Dressed in nothing but a brief pair of red and blue swimming trunks and an unbuttoned white shirt, he was an awesome sight. A little too sure of himself perhaps, but he oozed male allure that scratched her spot from ten metres away.

As she drew closer, her gaze skimmed his body. She felt her face flame, and her breath stuck in her throat as she looked to see if he'd noticed.

Of course he had.

'Good morning, Poppy. Would you like me to turn around?' His voice held an underlying thread of amusement that creased into laugh lines around his mouth as he smiled.

Yet another different Jake lived at the beach. She

hadn't met this side of him, and unfortunately he was dynamite. She had to get away from him.

Squaring her shoulders, she smiled apologetically. The heat in her cheeks felt hotter than the scorching sand beneath her feet. Even her ears felt hot.

He wasn't exactly looking at her in a platonic way either, and he wasn't embarrassed to show it. It made her stiffen her spine. She was damned if she'd let him see her squirming.

She gingerly picked the purse out of his hand and sent a small smile in his direction without meeting his eyes. 'Morning, Jake. Thanks for that.' It was more of a mumble.

Great one, Poppy, she mocked herself. You handled that well. Still off balance, she hurried to put some distance between them. Catching up to her smallest nephew, she held out her hand for his and set off again for the Nippers gathered around the blue lifesaving tent erected on the sand.

She cast a final glance back at the motionless figure as he mockingly lowered the megaphone and offered her a slight bow. 'Smart Alec,' she muttered, walking so fast that Simon almost tripped.

'Sorry, Simon.' She was grateful for Jake's assistance but she felt like a wind chime the way he jangled her nerves.

Finally she drew level with the tent and searched the sand for a good vantage place to set up camp. Sunday at Junior Lifesavers was usually fun, and it gave her sister and brother-in-law a child-free morning off together once a week. The day had to improve. She waved at her other two nephews and settled down to watch the races.

* * *

Jake had shaken his head when he'd seen the purse fall. He'd recognised Poppy's red hair as soon as she'd stepped onto the beach. He'd seen no sign of children in her house, so the boys were probably not hers. With a smile on his face he'd allowed her to walk on a short way while he'd savoured the swing of her hips under the loose cheesecloth top, before lifting the megaphone to his lips. He'd almost found it hard to talk he'd been smiling so broadly. He wasn't going to get involved but he could have some fun.

As a fully qualified lifesaving instructor, the local surf lifesaving club had jumped at his offer to help out when he could on Nippers days. He found himself drifting towards where Poppy was sitting. He hadn't quite started duty yet, and kidded himself that it was almost where he had to be. He watched one of her boys finish his race a respectable third.

Samuel, Poppy's eight-year-old nephew, fell on the sand beside her. He shaded his eyes from the sun to see her expression.

'Well run, Sam. How come you didn't swim all the way?' she teased. 'I saw you walking through the water when I'm sure it was deep enough to swim.'

'It's really hard work, Auntie Pop, you should try it.'

Poppy grinned back at the mischief in her nephew's eyes. 'I don't think they have races for adults, Sam.' They smiled at each other. They both knew she wouldn't want to enter anyway.

A sudden shadow fell over her, blocking the sun,

and she found herself staring up into Jake's brilliant blue eyes.

'Yes, we do. We can run one now. I'm one of the race co-ordinators and I think your idea of an adults' heat is great.' He was enjoying a huge joke and the amusement was mirrored in the crinkled laugh lines around his eyes.

Poppy decided his grin was evil. And his teeth were strong and white and ready to bite. So you stay away from him girl, she warned herself.

He stood there like Superman in tiny red and blue swim trunks, bronzed from the sun and dusted with glistening pale hairs. Poppy gulped.

She felt the clutch of her stomach muscles as one part of her couldn't help but respond to the sheer masculinity of him. It shocked her and she looked away quickly, hoping he hadn't read her body's response in her face.

Deal with it. The man made her think of sex. She was supposed to be cured of handsome men.

'See how many parents you can round up and I'll tell the other instructor,' he said blithely, and soared off.

'Superhero and super-painful,' she muttered. Breathless, she felt she had already swum a race, but one look at the glee in her oldest nephew's face showed there was no way out. Resolutely she stood up. Great. Thanks, Jake. She plastered a sickening smile on her face and went canvassing.

An adults' heat, that's right. Perhaps it would be a good idea to get it over and done with. She sidled up to the nearest mother, who hesitated but agreed.

'Never know when we'll have another chance!'

She was becoming more confident. 'It can't be too bad—the kids manage,' she said to another mother.

'Why not, indeed?'

There were eventually eight mothers, plus Poppy, and four fathers. The men would run later in case more turned up.

Hah! Thought Poppy. Bet they don't!

The mothers dawdled up to the start and huddled together, self-consciously pulling at costume straps and nervously joking about fifty metres not being too far.

Suddenly Jake appeared beside her.

'Didn't I tell you?' His face was expressionless except for those dancing eyes full of unholy amusement.

'For adults it's one hundred metres' beach run, then one hundred metres' swim around the second line of markers and then one hundred metres' beach run.' He looked innocent and added, 'In less than five minutes or you don't pass.'

Of course all the mothers glared at Poppy.

She'd kill him!

'Too late to back out now,' someone in the crowd hooted, and the grumbling contestants lined up for the start.

Poppy could hear the children cheering as she tried to run a hundred metres through the soft sand without slowing. It was a relief to splash into the shallow water and dive into the deeper water so that she could swim.

Several seasons ago she'd enjoyed swimming laps almost daily at the local baths and she'd felt confident that the swim leg, at least, would pose her no problem. But that had been in the pool and she'd only ever played in the waves before. Beach swimming was different.

Every time she tried to time her breathing to avoid the waves she misjudged it and was slapped in the face at the wrong time. Three strokes forward through the trough and the swell pushed her two strokes back. This was all Jake's fault. Coughing and spluttering, she doggedly swam on.

Fifty metres out to the marker seemed twice that far, and she was sure it was because she had to swim up the front and down the back of the waves. She'd kill him. Where was that stinking marker anyway?

She found it and headed back. If only she could catch a wave and body-surf in. After a few attempts she decided the waves had lousy timing and she had to swim, pull and stagger through the waves to the shore. Jake was in deep trouble.

'Hell,' she gasped. She'd forgotten the other beach run.

Then Poppy heard her nephews cheering and she saw the mother in front stagger up the beach and heard the one behind catching up.

The sand was soft and she hadn't realised it was such a steep slope from the water to past the high-tide mark.

The roaring of the kids was almost drowned out by the roaring in her ears, and she could hear herself wheezing, but she pushed on.

The fathers kindly clapped them up the straight and cheered as they crossed the line to fall in gasping, bedraggled heaps on the sand.

Poppy's nephews gathered round her, laughing and clapping her on the back.

Samuel gave her a cheeky grin. 'Well run, Auntie Pop, but you should have swum, not walked through the waves.'

Poppy threw a mock punch at him and collapsed back onto the sand with a breathless laugh, her breasts heaving from the exertion.

She saw Jake watching them with a smile on his face, and he appeared to be enjoying the view. His shadow fell across her face and a strong brown hand offered to help her up.

He grinned and his eyes travelled wickedly over her, admiring her body under the damp, iridescent green one-piece. A slower and more knowing smile grew in place of the grin and Poppy felt the heat spread up her stomach to harden her already upright nipples as her body responded.

Still keyed up from actually completing the course, she accepted his help but added, 'You aren't my favourite person.'

The grasp of his hand increased her awareness of him. She stopped smiling.

There it was again. This effect he had on her was too much. She disentangled her hands and brushed them together to wipe off the sand—and the tingling in her fingers.

Retreat seemed a sensible idea. 'Come on, boys, I need a towel.' She avoided meeting Jake's eyes and headed for their gear, with her three nephews trailing curiously behind.

As she packed the car for home Poppy rubbed a sandy hand over her brow as if to brush away the tension.

Every time her glance had strayed to Jake she'd caught his laughing eyes on her, always amused as if at some secret joke. The conflicting emotions she'd suffered on and off all morning had left her drained.

Aidan, six and serious, suddenly sat down beside the car and started to cry.

'What's wrong, darling?' Poppy crouched down beside him and put her arms around him.

'I've lost my Joe.' His eyes brimmed with tears and he looked beseechingly up at his aunt.

Poppy took a deep breath and rubbed her forehead again.

'OK, where was he last?'

GI Joe figures were one of Poppy's pet hates. The boy took him everywhere and managed to lose the toy at most places. It drove Poppy mad, but otherwise Aidan was a model child and she tried not to become too unglued when it happened.

'On the beach near the tent.' Aidan's eyes pleaded hopefully.

'I'll go, Auntie Pop.' Sam stood beside her.

'OK, love, dash back and have a look. I'll stay with the other two and watch you from here. At least the car's under a tree.'

She could see the Nippers' tent from where she sat and it took him ten minutes to find Joe. Her breath faltered as she saw him turn to make his way back to the car.

Damn. He was walking with Superman. Sam will have given him a life story by now. Poppy cringed at the thought. She climbed out of the car and stood beside it, waiting.

Aidan ran up to them. 'Did you find him, Sam?'

Samuel pulled the toy from behind his back and threw it to him. 'Don't lose him again.'

Aidan grinned happily and climbed into the car.

'Hello—again.' Her voice was cool, and was obvious even to Sam.

Jake held his hat in large, capable hands and his thick, curly hair looked to be trying to bounce out the flatness imposed by the hat.

Now his eyes were deep, deep blue, so dark they almost appeared black. You could drown in eyes like his. Sensual and wicked. Her own eyes widened as she realised the direction of her thoughts.

'Sam shouldn't talk to strange men.' The sarcasm was for Jake but Sam looked crestfallen. She had to smile and pretend it had been a joke.

'Jake is a doctor at my work. I meant "strange" as in funny, peculiar, Sam—only a strange man could make your aunt swim at Nippers!'

Sam laughed in relief and Jake raised his eyebrows mockingly.

'I'm glad you clarified that, Poppy.' There was more to that simple statement than she could read, but she tried to shrug it off.

Again, it was urgent that she get away. She needed space from this man.

'Look, Jake, thanks again for saving my purse this morning, but we have to go. I have to get the boys home to my sister's for lunch.'

He stepped back with a slight gesture of his hands

as if to say he wasn't stopping her, but he didn't make it any easier by moving away.

Ignore him, Poppy told herself. She made sure the seat belts were all secure in the back before climbing in. Then, before she could reach for the doorhandle, Jake had opened the car door, as if it was something he had always done, and she started to feel trapped. Trying to climb elegantly into an old Land Rover that didn't have the good manners to have a step proved as difficult as she'd feared it might.

She landed with a plop on the vinyl seat and bounced twice thanks to the speed of her ascent. She shot a look that dared him to laugh, but only his cheek twitched to mar his deadpan expression.

She automatically counted one, two, three heads in the back seat and started the engine. In her haste to get away she stalled the vehicle twice, and by the time Jake's face was becoming indistinguishable in the rear-view mirror she was grinding her teeth.

Jake felt the smile drain away from his face. Poppy represented everything he had come here to discredit and she should be raising his hackles, not his libido. He'd known where she was at any given time this morning. He'd done his job and had ensured the swimmers had been safe, but it was as if his peripheral vision had been reserved just for her. He was supposed to be avoiding this woman but couldn't seem to stay away from her. This was crazy.

There was something fundamental about her that lit him up like the man he'd once been. He really liked the way she'd dug in and run the race—and had still finished with a sense of humour.

He wanted to take her to some fancy restaurant with dim lights and dreamy music and just feel her against him—though she would probably prefer satay in a noisy café with tiled tables. All he had to do was figure out why it was so damned important he try.

Certainly, there were good reasons for staying away from her. Her nephew had said she was divorced; she was definitely not giving him the come-on; also, she was a midwife at the local hospital, and work problems he didn't need. But mostly he wished she wasn't into all that alternative medicine stuff. He hated it and he still had to find that woman his brother had stayed with. There just didn't seem to be as much time to devote to looking for her as he'd thought he'd have.

His mind drifted back to Poppy. Despite himself, he grinned as he remembered the way she'd said, 'You aren't my favourite person.' She made him smile. She was different to the private-school girls he'd grown up with in Grays Point, or the studious female doctors during medical training, but he liked her.

Life in a country valley might prove just the thing. Beach at one end and mountains at the other, and his work—which he loved—in the middle. And Poppy? He rubbed his chin where the bristles were already growing through after his shave that morning. He didn't want to think about her and how she fitted in.

CHAPTER FOUR

LUNCH at Jasmine's house was always noisy. The dogs were barking and Poppy ducked to avoid being hit with a football as it bounced off the verandah rail in front of her.

'Don't hit your aunt, guys.' Jasmine's gentle voice made Poppy smile.

'You should have caught that, woman.' Glen, Jasmine's husband, added with a laugh.

She raised her eyebrows at him. 'Just don't burn the sausages. There are no children kicking balls in my back yard. I haven't had the practice.'

'Well, there should be children playing ball.' Jasmine had that glint in her eye again. She reached over and picked up a celery stick and brandished it at her sister. 'When are you going to find yourself a man, get married again and see birth from the business end?'

A fleeting picture of Jake holding their child flicked in front of Poppy's eyes, and unconsciously she shook her head to banish the thought. Poppy picked up a celery stick of her own and held it up as if it were a microphone. She spoke slowly and clearly at it to impress the point on her sister, and on herself.

'I am not getting married again.' She thought of Phillip and Carolyn—they weren't married—and the bond they shared with their baby. She'd been married to Tyson and he would never have been like that. She looked at her sister, hoping to make her understand.

'Lately, I've been thinking that doesn't mean I don't want to have a child. Do I have to get married again to have a baby?' She munched on her 'microphone' and caught her brother-in-law's raised eyebrows. He grinned back at her.

'No offence to good husbands, Glen, but having no man is streets ahead of being married to the one I had. Maybe I could advertise. "Wanted—genetically healthy sperm donor for New Age but aging woman."' She laughed as if that had been a joke but they all knew her marriage had left scars.

'You're kidding. Gossip runs around this town like kids around the kids' ward. Get a boyfriend. What about the new paediatrician? I've heard he's single, and with his job he must love children.'

Poppy sighed. It had to come. She didn't want to talk about Jake with her sister. She definitely didn't want to get involved with another doctor. The guy was infiltrating her life like a local anaesthetic under the skin. He numbed the edges of the wound her ex-husband had made. She still wasn't sure if it was going to feel better or worse when the local wore off. 'Thanks, but I don't think I need to get involved with another doctor.'

'OK. So don't get involved. Have fun. Do the boy-girl thing and tease each other. At least stop comparing all men to the snake. You're both unattached and past the age of consent. Have a no-strings-attached sexual rampage.'

'Glen?' Poppy looked for help. 'Can't you stop your wife from making lewd suggestions.'

'Hell, no. It took me this long to train her.' The three of them laughed but Poppy was the first to sober.

'Leave it, Jasmine. I don't need to have a man in my life for it to be complete.'

Jasmine put up her hands in surrender. 'Fine, just don't be afraid to risk a little if one does come along. So, how was Nippers this morning? Sam said you earned your "S" badge for run-swim-run? Who conned you into that?' Jasmine looked utterly innocent.

Poppy felt her face flame, but she had to laugh at the memory. 'I didn't realise it would be so hard.' She glanced at Glen. No help there. She'd have to change the subject again. 'So when are we going to eat? All that exercise has made me ravenous.'

Three little boys appeared magically at the word 'eat' and the confusion that followed safely disposed of the conversation. For the moment.

Late that afternoon, Jasmine walked Poppy out to her Land Rover. 'Thanks for taking the boys. Just one question before you go. Who was the lifesaver? A man from your work, Sam said.'

'Jasmine!' Poppy tilted her head and glared. 'Thanks for lunch.' She shook her head and jumped up into the Land Rover.

Whew. Poppy accelerated down the drive to get away. She loved her sister dearly but since their mother's death she'd noticed that Jasmine had taken to worrying about her in a more maternal way.

Goodness knew why—she had enough children of her own to worry about.

With a squeak of springs and rattle of loose panels the old Land Rover rolled to a stop to settle ponderously under the giant jacaranda in front of her house. Poppy rested her head on the steering wheel and sighed, before opening the door to get out.

For the man watching from her front verandah, the car typified the contrasts he saw in this woman.

She touched a chord of response he found hard to fight. She alienated him with her radical leanings then the next moment she drew him with her zest for life and ability to make him laugh.

He shouldn't be here. This was crazy. He'd almost left just before she'd pulled up but something had made him wait. He'd gone home from the beach and had finally finished the last of the unpacking. He hated chaos and he should be at home, enjoying the neatness and order of his new home.

Jake had become used to his own company over the last couple of years and it felt alien to want to be with another person again.

But seeing Poppy at the beach today, it had jolted him. He'd fought it but had felt anxious and unsettled until he'd finally given in. Perhaps, having come to her house again, it would reinforce all the reasons they didn't suit each other.

Jake winced as she slammed the door of the old car—he'd never slammed a door in his life—and braced himself for her surprise. She bent down and scooped up a handful of purple bells off the grass to admire, before scattering them through her fingers. They were lovely. He hadn't noticed much about nature for the last couple of years and this woman had him seeing the flowers in less than a month.

An image of them both naked, making love on a carpet of fallen flowers, made him catch his breath. He shook his head and cleared his throat to attract her attention.

'Good afternoon.'

She'd have known that voice anywhere. Poppy frowned, disgusted at her brain fog, but this guy certainly seemed to short-circuit her synapses. She squinted up at him. What was he doing on her verandah?

'Hello, again. Aren't you the man who laughed at me today?' She watched his smile change his face from the somewhat forbidding doctor to the teasing lifesaver of earlier today. Her shoulders relaxed and she felt her body apparently melt. Where was that paper bag to put over his head so she could trust him?

'Who, me? Nah.' He grinned at her and patted the seat beside him. 'I found this really great seat and the view's pretty, too. Care to join me?'

Poppy tilted her head as if considering, but her mind was racing. What was he doing here? As she stepped over the rounds of river stone in the path towards him she couldn't help the flutter of awareness that tickled under her ribs. It wasn't fair for him to be so damn masculine. She had an irreverent thought—great gene pool. She had to duck her head to hide her smile.

'I might.' She felt his eyes on her and tried not to feel self-conscious as she sat down next to him.

'So, what brings you to such a non-conventional place?'

'I was wondering if you felt like sharing Chinese takeaway tonight.'

She shook her head very sadly. 'Gee. I'm pre-booked tonight—I've already defrosted a chicken. But thanks for the thought.'

'Is it a big chicken?' Jake tried to look innocent but couldn't help looking like a wolf.

Poppy laughed. 'No, *I* am. So you're not invited.'

He didn't say anything, just smiled and slid his hips across the seat until he rested against her, touching her at shoulder and thigh. As they gently swung backwards and forwards their legs touched at calf and knee, and then his fingers entwined in hers and she sighed. It felt so good.

She shouldn't encourage him to stay but it was no use. She kept thinking of her own sister telling her to have a no-strings-attached sexual rampage. The idea didn't seem so crazy with Jake here beside her. Yes, she was afraid—but there was something about when she was with Jake that made her ignore her common sense. What she really wanted was to wrap herself around him and breathe in the elusive masculine scent of him.

He looked back at her and put one finger gently under her chin to raise it. His finger stroked her cheek and his smile was gentle. 'Can we go inside?'

Poppy was in trouble. She'd turned into a big pink marshmallow and the problem was that it felt so damned good, being this mushy. If she invited this warm, funny Jake into her home it would be dangerous. But she'd have to be careful. There was no way they could ever have a serious relationship, given their huge ideological differences.

Also she needed to talk to him about her mother and James.

But the reality was that he looked so great and turned her knees to water, and she could feel the excitement bubbling away inside her. She tried to form a refusal but the words wouldn't come. Finally she gave a tiny shrug at her own weakness and gave in.

She stood up, then bent to lift a particularly ugly ceramic frog from beside the door to pull a key out from under it. She opened the door and slid the key back.

The look on Jake's face made her roll her eyes. He was horrified. 'Great security, Poppy. At least be a little less obvious with your hiding place.'

'Listen, Papa Bear, this is my house, and as the locks would break with a decent kick, anyway, I do it my way. Do you still want to come in?'

She watched him glance towards the big Land Rover resting in its bed of petals. She had no idea what he was thinking now.

'Yes, please.'

This time when he entered her home he was behind her. Right behind her.

Poppy could feel Jake's warmth against her back. It felt so good when he wrapped his arms around her and pulled her back against his body. He was big and solid and he made her tall, rounded frame feel fragile—something no other man had been able to do.

She finally stopped envying those tiny, helpless

women that men seemed to drool over. This was better.

He turned her slowly in his arms and they stood face to face, breath to breath, and savoured the moment.

Then his lips descended on hers, and they were firm and cleverly inquisitive. She sighed with bliss against him. His breath was fresh and warm as she breathed him in down to her toes. He nibbled her mouth and brushed her lips with increasing depth until they melded together and time receded. They swayed to some inner tune, their arms around each other as the kisses slowly became more hurried and then almost frantic before they sank to the carpet.

She felt him lift his hands to her hair and bury his hands in it as he pulled her face closer. Her heart was pounding like running feet on a pavement, and when he kissed along the delicate line of her jawbone and then up to her ears, as if he couldn't taste enough of her, she dragged in her breath.

She tilted her head back invitingly and he slid his lips down the line of her throat, barely touching her—yet his breath seemed to burn her skin. She shivered at the maddening sensation. Fighting for breath, she mumbled his name. 'Jake?'

'Hmm?' He lifted his head from her shoulder and smiled at her languorous expression.

'If you don't stop soon, I must warn you that I won't be able to invite you for tea.'

He glanced once more at the rapid rise and fall of her breasts and then lifted his eyes to hers. 'Is this a cooling-off period?'

He didn't look annoyed and Poppy snuggled

against him. 'Just intermission. Why do you make me feel like a dizzy teenager?'

Jake hugged her. 'You, too?' He rose to his feet and pulled her up effortlessly after him to stand again in the circle of his arms. 'This is where we started. Let's go find this chook.'

Jake was handy in the kitchen. His hands were everywhere. Poppy juggled preparing the chicken and slapping his hands away so she could concentrate. She giggled more in the next half-hour than she could remember over the last two years. Jake's sense of humour was wacky and his method of preparing vegetables bordered on the risqué. By the time they had filled the oven and set the table, the tension in the room was affecting them both.

The tiny kitchen seemed to be shrinking with every second they spent in there. It might be time to move to a larger room while they waited for the meal to cook. 'Let's go into the lounge. I'll grab the wine if you get the glasses.'

Poppy rummaged at the back of the fridge for the bottle, ostensibly finding it difficult to locate as she wriggled her bottom at him. She heard him stifle a groan and knock over one of the glasses. She grinned to herself, before straightening up. 'Here it is.'

She saw him rub his hand over his chin and draw in a deep breath. He gathered the glasses without looking at her and left the room. Poppy smiled. She hadn't realised there was such a teasing vamp inside her. Jake definitely brought out the worst—or maybe it was the best—in her.

This was fun. There was no way she was going

to get serious here, but maybe this boy-girl thing was what she needed, as Jasmine had said. As long as no one got hurt, and it stayed fun, she couldn't see why she shouldn't revel in the feelings he aroused in her. She felt as if she'd been in limbo for two years and hadn't realised it. And she was going to stay in control.

Jake was sprawled on the lounge. His hair was ruffled, as if he'd been raking it with his fingers, and she smoothed it with her free hand, before showing him the opened bottle. She sank down on the floor between his knees. A low table in the middle of the room held the glasses and she leaned forward to pour the golden wine.

Jake ran his hand down her spine and she arched against him before turning and handing him the glass.

'*You* are a tease.' He looked very relaxed and even quietly amused.

Poppy grinned and admitted it. 'Yep, but only with you. I've decided you bring out the worst in me.'

'If that's your worst, I can handle that. So how about putting down that glass, turning around and telling me why I feel like I've known you for ever and yet I don't know you at all?'

Poppy looked at him. 'Isn't that amazing? When I first saw you, you reminded me of someone I once knew.' Her stomach dropped as she realised what she's just said. She'd been meaning to bring it up but now that it was out she wished it unsaid. Their meetings had rolled from one point to another and she hadn't had time to think about how to broach the subject of James or her mother's role in the last few weeks of his life.

At Jake's quick intake of breath, she closed her eyes. She felt him rise off the lounge and tower over her. When she opened them, his concentrated stillness warned her that his mind was racing. 'What do you mean? Did you know my brother?' A sudden look of revulsion crossed his face. 'Were you the woman he stayed with?'

Lost for words, and not sure where to find them, Poppy stared at him.

'Answer me!' The cold-eyed stranger bore no resemblance to the laughing helper-hinderer in the kitchen. Had it been only ten minutes ago?

She closed her eyes briefly again and sighed. Then she opened than again and stood up beside him. 'No. It wasn't me.'

She watched Jake sag in relief and she bit her lip. Poppy hated subterfuge and she wouldn't resort to it. She felt cold all over but pushed herself to form the words, watching his face as she said them. 'It was my mother, Jake.'

Jake didn't say anything. He closed his eyes briefly and then gave her a curious half-smile. 'Thanks for being honest, anyway.' He grimaced.

Poppy opened her mouth to explain but he held up his hand.

'Don't. Please. Don't say anything.' He patted his pockets and she heard a key chink. 'I think I'll head home. Goodnight, Poppy.'

She stood without moving and listened to the sound of the front door as it gently shut. There was no sound of a car, and she hadn't seen one when she pulled up, so he must have walked to her house. Poppy pursed her lips and looked briefly at the ceiling as if for divine inspiration, before dragging her feet slowly into the kitchen. The smell of chicken made her feel sick.

She opened the kitchen window and turned the oven down. Jasmine could have the chicken tomorrow, but she'd finish cooking it so she didn't give her nephews salmonella poisoning. She gave a half laugh, half sob. What she really felt like doing was throwing the hapless bird out onto the back lawn.

Poppy wandered back through to the lounge room and puttered around, straightening cushions and picking up and laying down magazines. But she couldn't settle. She hadn't slept much the previous night and tonight didn't look as if it was going to be any better. Maybe a night staring mindlessly at the TV was the way to go? She frowned at the blank screen in front of her.

Or she could go to Jake's house and have it out with him. She sniffed. He had turned up on her doorstep without being asked. Having turned the idea over in her mind, she shrugged. What could he do? Throw her out? Shout? No, he wouldn't do that.

What if he needed more time to figure it all out? Then again, maybe he was really hurting. She accepted that there could be no relationship between them but she hated to think of him despising her mother. There was a slim chance that she could ease that by explaining the positive changes she'd seen in James while he'd stayed with Rose.

Poppy sighed and shut the kitchen window. Grabbing the cork for the wine, she pushed it into the bottle on the way out, before tucking it under her arm. She'd just go over there and see how he was. She wouldn't stay long.

The wind nearly lifted her off her feet as she pulled the front door closed behind her. The lovely sunny day was gone and had been replaced by a grey-skied storm front that gusted the petals off the grass and down the road.

It looked like rain, and Poppy shivered in her thin cheesecloth top. It seemed like days had passed since the beach this morning. She should really go back inside and shower and change. But she didn't. She climbed into the Land Rover and drove off down the road with her mind curiously empty of what she was going to say.

When she knocked at the door of the neat brick medical flats opposite the hospital her heart was thumping like a dog's tail on a wooden floor. Suddenly she panicked and decided this wasn't a good idea, but as she turned away the door opened and Jake was standing there.

He looked unsurprised to see her. She wondered if he might even have been hoping she would come.

'Come in, Poppy. You look cold.'

Actually, she was feeling more scared than cold. 'Are you OK, Jake?' Poppy searched his face.

He took the bottle and sat it on the hallway table before he turned his back on her and walked into the lounge room.

'No.' he said over his shoulder. 'I've just found out that the parent of a friend of mine is the person I've hated for three years. I suppose you've come to tell me how your mother did the right thing by James. So convince me!'

Ironically, his comment reminded Poppy of one of the first conversations they'd had. She tried for a little bit of lightness. 'My success would depend on whether you're open to reasonable argument or whether your mind is already made up, Doctor.'

His smile was more of a grimace. 'Now, where have I heard that before?'

He stood in front of the window with his arms folded across his chest.

Poppy sighed at his body language and tried to order her thoughts. This was what she'd hoped for when she'd come—she just wished she didn't feel that any future friendship with Jake might rest on her words. Taking a deep breath, she plunged in.

'I met James at Mum's house the day after he arrived. Your brother was a special guy, Jake, but he did look very stressed. He said he wanted time out to get his head together, and my mother taught him relaxation techniques, as well as prescribing Australian bush flower remedies to ease his symptoms.' She felt Jake move irritably beside her.

'And was that supposed to cure him.'

The wealth of bitterness in his softly spoken comment made Poppy grit her teeth and feel like shaking him. It was no use—she may as well go home. Then she sighed, deciding she'd try once more.

'She wasn't trying to cure him, Jake. James knew his life was measured in weeks. He wanted to have some quality and calmness in the last weeks of his life. I believe my mother gave him that.'

Jake unfolded his arms and started to pace. 'He

should have been in Sydney, having treatment.' He reached the other side of the small room and turned back to face her. 'They could have extended his time. He should have tried. I had the best oncologists in the country lined up.'

Poppy ached for his pain and searched for the right words. 'Listen to yourself. Even you're using phrases like "extended his time". What sort of quality of life would he have had just to gain even a few weeks?' She stared into his face, willing him to understand. 'Jake?' But she could tell he wasn't listening.

'He wasted his chance at life here.' He curled his lip. 'Getting his head together.'

'You're still angry with your brother for dying. There comes a time when you have to let people go, let them choose for themselves, Jake. He chose to go his way!'

He stopped pacing and looked at Poppy. 'And your mother encouraged him.' He turned away again.

'Hello? Jake? You're missing the point and back to looking for blame.' Jake still wasn't listening and she felt like throwing something at him.

'I don't think I want to meet her.'

Her shoulders dropped. He was hopeless.

'You won't. She's dead.' The words were quietly spoken and Jake froze with his back to her.

Poppy stood up and her voice was strong and clear. 'But she lives in me, Jake. I am very proud of the help Mum gave to people like your brother. Every time you look at me you're going to have to deal with that—or don't come near me. Now it's my turn to go home.' She patted his shoulder and walked past him out the door. He didn't call her back.

It was sheeting with rain as she drove home, and the trees at the side of the road were whipping back and forth. It suited her mood. Broken branches skittered across the road with each gust. The small car in front of her was being buffeted by the strength of the wind.

Thank goodness for solid old cars, Poppy thought as she ploughed along in the semi-darkness, crunching over the debris in the Land Rover. Pulling up outside her house, she wiped her eyes with the back of her hand and realised that she'd been crying. She sat there with her hands on the cold steering wheel.

Damn Jake. She didn't need this emotional seesaw. This was supposed to be fun. Seeing him so twisted with unresolved grief and anger, she'd tried to do something for him. Her mother had behaved in the best interests of James, and until Jake could cope with that Poppy was better with him out of her life. She'd done the right thing. Hadn't she?

Dropping her hand to the car doorhandle, she pushed against the wind. Her hair whipped around her face. She ducked her head and sprinted up the path, knocking the frog over in her haste to get into the house. She leaned back against the door once she was safely inside, and sighed.

But they fitted so well together and she loved Jake's sense of humour when his demons were sleeping. It would have been wonderful to be curled up with him in bed with the wild storm outside.

Damn.

CHAPTER FIVE

POPPY carefully returned the framed photograph of her mother to the hall table. 'Two years today. I'm so sorry you can't see the changes we've made for the better at work—or maybe you can.' Poppy swallowed the lump in her throat and shut the door behind her. The sky was blood red and the air was muggy with the promise of heat as she walked to work.

There was no one at the nurses' station when she stepped into the ward to start her shift and one of the birthing-room doors was shut. Something was going on. She took a deep breath before she knocked quietly and pushed open the door.

Poppy had seen too many similar scenes not to recognise the presence of bad news. Jake was leaning tiredly against the wall, speaking into the ward phone. Dr Gates nodded and walked past her to leave the room. The labouring woman's worried husband leaned consolingly towards his wife.

Jake raised his eyebrows at her in recognition as if to say, And we thought we had worries.

The night sister grimaced in her direction, obviously glad to see Poppy and the end of her own shift, but Poppy's gaze was drawn to the young mother. It was Therese, one of the young mums who'd attended the eight weeks of Poppy's antenatal classes.

Therese looked tragically glad to see Poppy's familiar face.

Poppy moved to the side of the bed next to Mark, Therese's husband, and took the girl's hand in hers.

'Hi, Therese, Mark.' She smiled gently and received a poor imitation of a smile in reply.

'They think there's something wrong with our baby, Poppy.' Mark's voice wobbled as he tried hard to speak clearly and he turned away to hide his face.

Poppy sat on the side of the bed close to Therese and squeezed her hand. 'What sort of wrong, sweetheart?'

Therese swallowed but couldn't get the words out.

'The child appears to be anencephalic.' Jake's quiet voice fell into the silence, and Poppy's eyes met his.

It was tragic news. A baby with anencephaly—meaning without a brain—couldn't live outside the uterus. Once born, when the mother stopped supplying all the nutrients, oxygen and bodily functions required to sustain life, the child would die. A time when birth meant death. Poppy's heart went out to the parents. And to the child who would never know the joys of life. But there would be time to say goodbye later. She squeezed Therese's hand again and met her eyes.

'Are you in much pain at the moment?'

The young woman shook her head. 'It's bearable.'

Poppy nodded. 'I'll just slip out and Night Sister will give me the hand-over report. I'll be back in a few minutes to stay with you both. OK?' The young couple nodded and Poppy and the night sister walked towards the door. She looked a question at

Jake. He shook his head and closed his eyes as he leaned against the wall.

Back at the nurses' station the junior midwife, Julie, had arrived. Poppy and Julie listened as Night Sister ran quickly through the patients on the ward and then Therese's case. She outlined the reasons for the diagnosis.

'She had her first ultrasound yesterday and it is strongly suggestive of anencephaly. Her blood test early in pregnancy was abnormal, but Therese and Mark both said they still wanted to go through with the pregnancy and refused further tests until she had a small bleed yesterday.'

Poppy shook her head. Poor Therese and Mark.

'She's in established labour, and Dr Gates has just done a vaginal examination. She's five centimetres dilated and he feels there's an unusual descending part. It's ominously consistent, I'm afraid.'

Poppy sighed. 'OK. How long has Dr Sheppard been here?'

'Before definite diagnosis, the graph of baby's heart rate was erratic, and Dr Gates was going to do a Caesarean until he woke up the radiographer for the results of the ultrasound. Dr Sheppard was called in before that at five a.m. He's staying until delivery, he said.'

Poppy fretted. Don't make it harder, Jake. Surely there wouldn't be any attempts to prolong life beyond the baby's ability to die peacefully. 'What are his thoughts on resuscitation?'

The night sister looked nervously at Poppy. She was well aware of Poppy's views. She looked away.

'He said that as soon as the baby is born he would transfer it to the nursery.'

Poppy closed her eyes and then lifted her chin. 'Even if it's anencephaly? What for? What about the parents?'

Night Sister grimaced wryly. 'I'll leave you two to sort that one out. I'll stick my head in to say goodbye to Therese and Mark and then I'm off to bed. If I can sleep, that is.' She rose wearily and handed over the keys to the drug cupboard. Poppy gave the drooping girl a quick hug. 'You've done a great job. Sleep well.'

Slipping the drug keys into her pocket, she looked up at the junior midwife. 'If you don't mind, I'll take the birthing room and you take the ward, Julie.'

Julie nodded in relief and bustled off down the ward to check on the mothers and their babies.

Poppy headed purposefully down the corridor. As she slipped inside the room, Therese was breathing steadily through a contraction. She appeared well controlled and Mark was coaching her, gently matching his breathing to hers. Poppy smiled in congratulation at both of them and signalled with her fingers that she would be back in two minutes.

'Dr Sheppard.' She watched Jake open his eyes. For once she wasn't interested in their blueness. 'Would you mind if I speak to you outside, please?'

Jake straightened up off the wall and looked down at Poppy. For a moment she thought he wasn't going to budge, then he shrugged his shoulders and followed her through the door. They walked along to the fire-exit door, where they couldn't be overheard, while Poppy marshalled her thoughts.

'Yes, Sister?'

She could see he wasn't going to help her and she closed her eyes at his obtuseness. He was just like Tyson.

Poppy took care with the words she chose. 'Do you agree with Dr Gates that this baby is an anencephalic baby?'

'Yes, I would say that is the most likely scenario.'

'What were your plans for the baby following diagnosis at delivery, Doctor?' Poppy knew that while the parents had the ultimate decision, they were vulnerable. Unwittingly, Jake, as the paediatrician, could influence them to allow the baby to be taken to the nursery.

He frowned and dropped the formality. 'The child would go to the nursery for oxygen. It may live longer with that. Just until it passes away, Poppy. Why?'

'Don't you see, Jake? That would rob the parents of the only sharing of life, apart from the kicks in Therese's womb, they will have with this child. The length of life isn't really an issue here. This family will gain more if their child dies in their arms. Not yours or mine or in a crib. The baby isn't perfect but remains their child and holds all their dreams. The three of them need and deserve to spend every second they can together as a family.'

Poppy couldn't begin to imagine how terrible it would be to have a baby taken from you when you knew it would die while it was away. Why couldn't Jake see that?

He stared at her and then looked away into the distance as he spoke to himself. 'Not do anything?

What can I do to make a difference?' He rested the flat of his hand against the wall and then stood up straight to look at Poppy. 'Nothing, of course.'

Poppy was watching his face but couldn't read the expression in his eyes. 'Baby will stay with the parents as long as they want. It's their decision.'

She knew it must have been hard for him to even think of not treating the baby, and she sighed in relief. Thank God. He really did understand. She felt the tears pricking at the back of her eyes and blinked. It seemed that every time she could really dislike this man, he surprised her.

'Thank you. I'll go back in. Why don't you make yourself a coffee? You look tired.' Poppy wanted to stamp her foot at herself. Now she sounded like the little woman.

She turned away before she said anything else and slipped back into the room, but her step was lighter. Now she had more chance to help foster those beautiful moments that Therese and Mark would treasure in the years to come when they thought of their first-born.

The labour was hard but mercifully swift. The air of disaster, while still devastating, had lifted slightly. With her own tears held back, Poppy encouraged the parents to look forward to the little time they would have with their baby. By lunchtime it was all over. Baby Dray was born at 8 a.m. and died in his mother's arms at 9:50 a.m.

He stayed with his parents until later that afternoon, wearing a beribboned bonnet to shield his misshapen head and dressed in an exquisitely knitted dress and jacket. He had his father's nose.

Photographs and hand- and footprints were taken and a lock of hair saved for his album.

Jake had kept his word and once it had been proved conclusively that the baby wouldn't survive, he'd faded away to allow the parents privacy with their son. It had been an emotional time for everyone, but by the end of the day Poppy knew that she'd given the best care she could have in the circumstances. In the short time he'd lived, Baby Dray had touched the lives of all the people present, and Poppy felt privileged to have been one of them.

Walking home that afternoon, Poppy untied the band from her hair to let the wind blow through it. The sun seemed brighter and the view from the lookout she passed on the way home seemed clearer than this morning.

She phoned Jasmine for sympathy, refused an invitation to have the evening meal with them and shared a few special memories of their mother before she hung up.

She needed to soak in a bath silky with bath oil and the scent of the calming blend her mother had always used. She was tired, bone-sappingly weary and mentally fragile. A short while later she stepped out of the bath and wrapped her bath sheet around and around herself as if to ward off the sudden heaviness of her thoughts.

It was at times like this that she acknowledged that sometimes being alone wasn't always wonderful. What she really needed was a big, warm, enveloping cuddle! An image of herself in Jake's arms flashed into her mind before she pushed it away. What was Jake doing now? She smiled wryly to herself. The guy probably hadn't given her a thought.

She hardly knew the man and yet she felt as if she'd finally found someone she could trust. To a certain extent. As much as you could trust any man. Her father had died in Vietnam and she'd never even met him.

She'd married Tyson and he'd left when she'd needed him. Staring at the figure in the mirror, she forced herself to lift her shoulders and stand up straight. Deal with it, woman. You can stand on your own.

Jake couldn't shake the image of Poppy from his thoughts. Without having made a conscious decision, he found himself outside her door.

Things weren't turning out like he'd thought they would. He'd come to this town to do some unobtrusive detective work and maybe discover something he could hold against the woman with whom his brother had stayed to stop her practising.

His parents had been against it from the start, but his bitterness had bleached the colour from his life. Now there were more complications, and the idea of attacking the credibility of Poppy's mother wasn't as palatable. He still distrusted holistic medicine but he couldn't summon up the hatred he'd once felt.

Jake paused, before knocking on Poppy's door. What if someone from work was the last person she wanted to see? Was he the last person she wanted to see? He shrugged. All he knew was that he wanted to hold more than her image and he hoped she was home. He knocked.

* * *

Poppy knew it was Jake. She could stand on her own but it looked as if she might not have to. She forgot about the unglamorous towel—she didn't need to be combed and tidied. What she did need was Jake. When she opened the door he walked into her house and she stepped into his arms. Strong, warm arms wrapped around her and he hugged her to him, then pushed her gently further into the house, before shutting the door behind him.

Poppy sighed and the depth of her relief was mirrored in the instant enfolding of Jake's arms around her. They stood in the hallway and Poppy closed her eyes, gently breathing in the scent of his skin as she buried her nose in the V of his shirt.

He smelt like warm toast on a winter's night, and his chest hairs tickled her nose as if they had been grown there for just that purpose. She hugged him tighter and breathed his essence deeper into her body.

Poppy could almost feel the strength from his body recharging hers. Relaxing against him, she closed her eyes. He was like an elixir and now, with his chin resting in her hair and his arms wrapped around her, she could feel her energy returning as she savoured the circle of his arms. She fitted perfectly. Jake demanded nothing in return. Just stood there, giving her the big, warm, enveloping hug she needed. He was there to meet her needs—not his. His chest vibrated under her cheek as he spoke.

'When you called me out of that birthing unit my first thought was, Surely this isn't the time for dim lights and aromatherapy. I was irritable from lack of sleep and not very gracious. I wonder what you'd have done if I'd said, ''No, I'll stay here''!'

She smiled mistily up at him. 'Probably tried to pull you by the ear.'

They both smiled at the mental picture.

Jake squeezed her gently again. 'The passion and clarity of your thinking stunned me. I felt stupid and callous for not thinking of it myself. I work on the medical rationale of preserving life at all costs—I made an oath to follow that. But this was one of those times when it wasn't so black and white.

Poppy didn't want to talk about that now.

'Jake?' The muffled voice drifted up from his chest. His face softened.

'Yes, Poppy?'

'Would you take me to bed, please?'

'That's a hard one.' He smiled. 'But I think I could manage it.' He picked her up, still wrapped in the towel, and she felt fragile and cherished against his chest. She kept her eyes closed and nose buried as much as the change in the position would allow until he lowered her gently onto the bed. Then she looked up slowly as if waking from a trance.

'His eyes adored her.' The words of a song floated through her head and had never seemed so relevant. She watched the change in Jake's expression and felt her own body respond to the briny scent of the storm to come.

'Look at you.' His voice was husky. 'You lie there on some wildflower-covered quilt, with the towel rucked on one hip and the end tucked into the secret valley between your breasts.' His finger flipped out the tuck holding the towel together and it slid apart to reveal her nakedness.

Poppy gloried in her power to slip past his control, and reached up to pull him down beside her until his head lay turned to hers, and they kissed. This was right. The time, the place, the need. She didn't doubt that in some fundamental way this man was her soul mate. Her destiny. No matter how long or short their time together, she would never regret this night.

The kiss started gently. Almost like dew, it was soft and imperceptible. More of a breath than a kiss. Then, like the first drops of rain, it moistened them with wonder. Like a summer shower, sprinkling their skins in larger droplets until each deluged the other in increasing ferocity. Until the storm was upon them.

Poppy gasped for breath and they broke apart. She could see her own awe reflected in Jake's eyes as they stared at each other, bemused by the power they had unleashed. She watched, mesmerised, as his mouth descended on hers once more and she was lost. Again.

Her hands were behind his head, laced in his hair, and her body was arched against his as they pressed their bodies as close as they could.

But it wasn't enough. She pulled away again and rolled off the bed. The towel stayed behind and she gloried in the heated flare in his eyes as he leaned on one elbow, admiring the view.

'Would you, please, stand up so I can get rid of your damn clothes, Jake?' Poppy's voice was husky with urgency and he responded with suitable speed.

Jake helped her and she was glad. Once naked, he pulled her body against his and wrapped his arms around her. They stood there, the millions of nerve endings in their skins seeming to scream out in pleasure at the contact. His chest was as awesome as she remembered and she buried her face against it.

The springy swirls of black hair in the hollow of his neck tantalised her tongue with their softness. He tasted wonderful. The world beyond her room was gone. There was just her and Jake and the taste, smell and feel of their bodies together.

His strong hands slid down her back, kneading the muscles and curves on their way until they settled, cupping her buttocks and grinding her cheeks together teasingly. He lifted her effortlessly until her mouth was level with his, and there was something primal in his ability to do so.

He made her feel so feminine that she wanted to melt, and a tiny sound in her throat was answered with a plundering kiss that seemed to sear her soul.

Poppy clung to his shoulders for stability in a world that shuddered around her, and their breathing gasped in and out.

She felt him turn back to the bed and when he lowered her feet to the floor the bed against the back of her legs tipped her backwards and she lay, open and inviting, below him.

He knelt, and his strong hands slowly pulled their two bodies together.

It was so right. So perfect. She felt the tears pricking at the back of her eyes, and when Jake leaned forward and covered her mouth with his, the world tilted into a final whirlpool of passion that made her feel as if some small part of each of them were joined for ever.

Afterwards, she lay with her head over his heart, one leg caught between his, entwined and cherished and soft with release.

It would have been magic to have stayed like that for ever, but Poppy considered herself a realist. Life wasn't like that.

She was genuinely grateful to Jake for this brief window into a wondrous world. She would have hated to have been on her deathbed and never have experienced the last hour. She jolted out of that train of thought. Don't be morbid, Poppy.

She slipped her leg out from between Jake's and, despite an initial tightening of his arms around her, Jake let her go.

She didn't look at his expression. 'I'm hungry. Stay here and I'll bring us back something to eat.' She leaned over, dropped a kiss on his lips and slid out of bed. She shrugged into his shirt and unconsciously breathed his subtle intoxicating smell from the collar as it lay against her cheek.

Poppy could feel his eyes on her neck as she left the room. Keep it light, she told herself, but she knew it was going to be harder than she thought.

Bustling around in the kitchen, preparing a tray of breadsticks, cheese and chicken salad, and uncorking a bottle of Chardonnay she had at the back of the fridge, her heart was arguing with her common sense.

Poppy was scared. She'd needed Jake tonight and he'd been there. But she didn't want to need anyone.

Tyson had taken more than he'd given and the cost had been too great.

She wasn't going to rely on any man. Even if she did fit Jake's body like a key in the lock of life. They could be friends. Lovers. But she wasn't going to rely on a commitment that was meaningless. Her life was too good and it was too dangerous to feel this way. It was better to face facts and enjoy what was there without dreaming.

Her skin prickled and she looked up to see Jake lounging against the kitchen door. A small hiccup of laughter escaped as she surveyed his attire. He was wearing her dressing gown and he could hardly move his muscular arms because it was so tight. The mischievous light in his eyes drew her into his arms to lean against him.

'As you're wearing my shirt it's only fair that I wear something of yours.' He held her away so that she could see him breathe deeply into the collar of the gown and pantomime a beatific expression. She punched him gently in the chest and then burst out laughing.

'So, does this mean you're trying to tell me you cross-dress, Dr Sheppard?'

'I don't think you'll have to worry about it. I find it a bit restrictive.' His face grew serious. 'What's wrong, Poppy?'

'Nothing's wrong, Jake. Come back to bed.' He studied her face and she turned away, ostensibly to retrieve the platter of food. 'If you can bring the wine…'

Jake hooked the wine bottle and two glasses in one hand and followed her through into the bedroom. He savoured the cheeky peep of her bare buttocks under the flaps of his shirt. She drove him insane. One minute she was like Mata Hari and the next he felt shut out. Now she was lighting one of those damn burner things he hated. It didn't smell bad but it made him think of his brother and the waste of life.

He really had to come to grips with that. And Poppy's mother being involved. The whole alternative issue. Not tonight, though. He couldn't face rehashing it all at the moment. He could hear the wind chimes outside the window. When Poppy turned on the stereo and he heard the Pan flutes it was too much. It was almost as if she was deliberately emphasising their differences.

He put the wine down and moved to where she had her back turned to him. His arms caressed her shoulders and he leaned down to kiss her softly on the neck.

'The mood's gone, hasn't it?' she said, and he hugged her back against him.

'It's been a big day. We're both tired. Let's have a rain check on the picnic in bed. Something to look forward to.'

He tried not to grimace as he found himself staring at the oil burner. Poppy saw him and he watched her face change. She didn't launch into the advantages of essential oils but shrugged her shoulders delicately and offered him his clothes with a wry smile.

They dressed together like an old married couple and Jake marvelled at the lack of constraint where it could have been awkward. She was unique. He had to admit that.

He kissed her cheek at the door but he could feel the distance between them. Hearing the door shut as he walked down her path, he wondered why he didn't feel relieved that she hadn't demanded what he wasn't ready to give. Might never be ready to give.

He smacked his forehead at his own weakness. How could he forget all the reasons he shouldn't be with this woman. The last five minutes had underlined just some of them. He needed to distance himself from her right now before he was in so deep he couldn't get out.

Jake hadn't slept well. He couldn't believe how stupid he'd been, not even taking precautions. Kicking the twisted sheet out from under his leg, he stretched out naked to glare at the ceiling, his hands under his head. He ached with memories, and wanted to lose himself in Poppy again. And it worried him.

What was he doing? Comforting a friend was one thing, but there had been nothing friendly in the storm he and Poppy had created. It had taken until well into the early hours before he'd finally fallen asleep, and this morning she was still the first thing on his mind.

He wasn't going anywhere near her today and he would be very careful to keep his distance in the future. It would be better for her in the long run. He was relieved she wasn't demanding anything.

Jake decided he needed a cold shower and a big dose of work.

* * *

'So, you've taken the general patients and I get the obstetric ones, eh?' There was something about Dr Harvey that rubbed Jake up the wrong way.

With Dr Gates down with appendicitis, Jake had offered to take over some of the inpatient load, even though it had been years since he'd cared for adults. Maybe that was why he felt irritated and it wasn't the fault of the visiting obstetrician himself.

The man was up for a month's holiday relief from Sydney. He was polite, even flattering towards Jake's credentials, implying that Jake was too qualified for this small hospital.

A month ago Jake would probably have agreed, but the place was growing on him and the thought made him feel vaguely disloyal. Dr Harvey had worked there before and knew the staff, but Jake had the feeling he hadn't been popular. Dr Harvey was filling out sick certificates when Jake escaped from the medical ward. It felt good to shake the other doctor off.

Jake drifted towards the maternity unit. 'Good morning, Cassandra.' He smiled at Poppy's friend and glanced over her shoulder down the ward, frowning as he saw another midwife enter one of the birthing units. Poppy wasn't there. 'All the kids fine?'

'Good morning, Dr Sheppard—I mean Jake. No problems for you.' Jake heard the corridor door open behind him and both smiles faded as they saw who'd come in.

'Excuse me, Jake, I have to make a phone call.'

He watched Sandy turn and walk stiffly away from him just as Dr Harvey appeared at his shoulder.

'This place hasn't changed.' The sneer in Dr Harvey's voice confirmed Jake's dislike of the man. He shrugged. Internal politics. It wasn't his problem.

He needed to see Poppy, he thought, grimacing. So much for his early morning thoughts. Maybe he needed to see her in normal circumstances, away from the dramas in the hospital and certainly nowhere near her house—or her bedroom. If they sat down together they probably wouldn't have anything in common.

'If anyone needs me, I'll be on my pager.' He nodded at the other man and strode towards the door.

CHAPTER SIX

THERE were something like thirty-two days a year when a woman could get pregnant, and Poppy was pretty sure it hadn't been yesterday—but they would have to be more careful. Next time. She was crazy. There was absolutely no sense at all in getting involved with Jake Sheppard. The trouble was, when he was there she just didn't care.

Her skin tingled at the thought. They might have differences in opinion, but the chemistry between their bodies couldn't be denied. Jake made her feel the most desirable, sexy, feminine woman on the planet—and he only had to look at her. When he worshipped her with his hands and mouth, he made her want to share parts of herself that no one had ever known, made her confident that whatever she did for him would be wonderful.

Poppy could feel the last shreds of inadequacy left from her marriage to Tyson dimming into obscurity. The marriage had lasted for three years. She'd never thought she'd be glad she hadn't fallen pregnant. In fact, she remembered days when she would have given anything to have had Tyson's baby.

She winced. Imagine being tied to a man who made you feel less of a woman. Even when married to him, sleeping with Tyson had made her feel as if there had been rules to be obeyed. Yet with Jake she felt like a deliciously wanton princess. But she wasn't getting tied to him either.

Then the phone rang.

Poppy dropped the phone into its cradle a few minutes later with a feeling of distaste. Damn. Tyson was back in town. She felt like having another shower. Sandy had never liked her ex-husband and been apologetic on the phone, not wanting to spoil Poppy's day off. But it would be just like the snake to sleaze up for a free meal if he caught her off guard.

The doorbell rang and Poppy glared at it. That had been fast. Short shrift is what you're getting, boyo, she vowed as she marched to the front door and threw it open.

'Yes?'

The quick-fire question wasn't the greeting Jake had expected, judging by the way he stiffened. Poppy felt like a fool.

'I'm sorry, Jake. I thought you were someone else.'

'This is a quick visit but if it's not a good time…?' He shrugged and turned to leave but she rested her hand on his arm to stop him.

'Please, stay. I'll make a coffee.' She smiled. 'And I promise, no Pan flutes this early in the morning.'

'So you noticed? No coffee thanks, Poppy.' If she hadn't known better she'd have said he was nervous. 'Will you have dinner with me on Wednesday night? I'm on call the next two nights.'

She frowned at the strange expression on his face

but answered easily enough. 'I'd like that. What time and where were you planning?'

'Seven, and I thought we'd try out of town—the Beach Hut, beside the surf club. Maybe go for a walk after the meal. On the beach?'

'That sounds wonderful, Jake.' He still looked strange. 'Thank you.' She couldn't resist, and leaned across to kiss his lips briefly before he turned and left.

Poppy ran her tongue lightly over her lips and savoured the lingering tang of his aftershave against her cheek. Keep it cool. Boy-girl stuff. Nothing serious. She leaned against the door frame and waved as he slid his large frame behind the wheel of his white Mercedes saloon. She felt the smile tug at the corner of her mouth. The car was a perfect example of their differences.

If she had a choice of car she would lean towards a new Range Rover or at least a sporty four-wheel-drive with a hood to push back. She looked across at her trusty old Land Rover and decided to get out for the day. She'd explode if she didn't burn off some of this energy. A drive to Dorrigo to hike the waterfall trail in the national park was what she needed. She quickly calculated the time. With the four-hour walk, plus the drive, she could be back by dark. It would be worth it for the sense of peace that she never failed to find in the rain forest. And Tyson wouldn't find her there.

The next afternoon at work, Poppy closed the birthing-unit door on the relaxation music and leaned against it. She really would have liked to have slipped back into the calm, peaceful atmosphere and avoid Tyson. The obstetrician replacing poor Dr Gates had to be her ex-husband. Damn. She stiffened her shoulders. She could deal with him for one month.

'Are you still encouraging this rubbish?'

Listening to the sneer in his voice, it made her close her eyes briefly. 'Just like old times, Tyson.' Poppy smiled through gritted teeth and wondered how she'd once thought she would love him for ever—if it had ever been love. The guy was a jerk. She shook her head in amazement and drew him down the corridor away from the labouring woman's room, feeling vaguely that he might contaminate the aura surrounding the birth.

'Page me when she's ready to have the baby and I'll come back to deliver it.' His smug I'll-save-the-world voice grated on her ears.

'Sure.' Poppy held her fingers crossed behind her back. It would be terrible if he was thirty seconds late for the delivery. Still, these things happened.

She felt his hand on her arm and she stopped to face him. He was at least six feet tall, but in Poppy's eyes he was only half a man. She realised she was comparing him to Jake. Jake could squash him like an ant. Poppy indulged herself in the thought, like a schoolchild's my-dad's-bigger-than-your-dad boast.

He stared down her uniform front. 'You look great—different, but great. Poppy, I've missed you.'

Poppy hoped her mouth hadn't fallen open. 'Jerk' was too soft a word. Creep. Moron. She shook his hand off her arm.

'How about dinner with your old man while I'm in town?' He crinkled his eyes at her. She'd never realised that it made him look sly. Heck, she used to think it was sexy.

She realised how ridiculous he was, and suddenly she felt liberated from all the negative feelings she'd harboured. He wasn't even worth getting angry with. 'Ex, Tyson. And how is your wife?'

'Come on, Poppy. For old times' sake.'

Poppy stepped up close to him and narrowed her eyes. He really thought she would be interested in spending time with him. She couldn't believe it. She poked him in the chest and enunciated slowly and clearly, 'No, I do not want to have dinner with you. Never. Ever. Grow up, Tyson. Oh, and give my regards to your poor wife.'

Jake had felt restless all day. His brilliant idea had backfired. Arranging an across-the-table discussion with Poppy was supposed to prove how little they had in common. And that would have been that. But this was crazy. After he'd booked the restaurant, Jake had realised that this was the first time he'd asked a woman out alone since his wife had died. He'd been no recluse and had accepted invitations when they'd come, but to actually plan and look forward to an evening of conversation was a big step. And he *was* looking forward to it. He'd nearly blown the invitation, too.

It still rankled how nervous he'd been. His usual control had slipped badly and he didn't like it. He'd even decided not to ask her in the end—just as he'd heard his voice asking the question. Then he'd laid out plans he hadn't realised he'd even made.

The irony was that he and Poppy had already been together in the true sense of the word—so why was he still nervous about a date? Unfortunately, he had no idea what was in her mind and he needed to know. Which direction would she take next? She was so different from anyone he had ever known and she confused and unsettled him.

A wry grin twisted his lips in acknowledgement. When he thought about her, some other, less controlled Jake took over. She turned him on like no other woman ever had. He winced with guilt. Not even in the early days of his marriage had he felt like this.

This business with her mother's involvement with James's death was something he knew he would have to work through, but it wasn't easy. Now that he knew who the woman was he supposed he could leave and go back to Sydney again.

His parents had thought him mad, uprooting himself from his practice and family to 'irrationally pursue' some crazy vengeance that wouldn't bring back his brother from the dead.

Maybe they were right and he had been mad with grief. Or had it been fated that he come here to free his mind from the destructive bitterness that had drained him for the last three years? When it all came down to reality, how much of that lifting of spirit was because of Poppy?

He pushed open the door to Maternity. She was working this afternoon and should be around the ward somewhere.

When Jake saw Poppy playing with Dr Harvey's shirt in the corridor, he felt the blow as if someone had punched him. Then she was coming towards him with that hundred-watt smile as if he was just the person she was waiting for. Maybe he wasn't ready to re-enter the world of dating and mating. She didn't look one bit guilty at being caught either. Without moving, he watched Harvey follow her up the corridor. The guy even tilted his head to watch the way her uniform clung.

Poppy was saying something about the neonatal nursery but Jake wasn't listening. He was staring at Harvey. Hating him. Visualising taking him by the throat and lifting him off the ground and maybe slamming his head against the pastel wall a couple of times. Jake swallowed the rage in his throat. Unhealthy stuff here, Sheppard. Jake blinked and dragged his eyes away from the other man to Poppy.

'So the new cribs work fine.'

'Sorry. Drifted off for a minute.' Jake stared hard at her.

Poppy tilted her head. 'You OK, Jake?'

'Speaking of drifting, check out the music and the stink in the labour ward. That stuff would drift you into next year.' They both turned to Dr Harvey. Jake heard Poppy sigh and he frowned. Suddenly—and he wasn't quite sure how it had happened—he was an advocate for holistic midwifery.

'Really? Complementary therapies are being used across the board in a lot of hospitals now. I think the midwives here do a great job in helping the mothers to relax.'

Poppy was staring at him in disbelief and Dr Harvey was curling his lip.

'So? Big deal. How does it help clinically? It's all mumbo-jumbo and sometimes it's dangerous. Give me an example of a benefit, clinically.'

So this was what Poppy came up against all the time. Jake saw her tense for battle but he stepped in first. 'Clinically...' he stared at the smaller man '...fewer narcotic drugs are used in labour and I haven't seen a drugged baby that needed reversal since I came here. Can you say the same at your hospital in Sydney?'

He watched with contempt as Dr Harvey back-pedalled.

'Yeah, there's that.' He glanced at his Rolex watch. 'Sorry, I'd love to continue this, but I have an appointment. Have to go. See you later, Poppy, love.' He smirked at them both and sauntered down the corridor.

'Poppy, love? What a jerk!'

Jake heard her words and saw her shake her head, but he didn't feel like smiling back at her. Now that Dr Harvey had gone, he had time to think back on Poppy flirting with that idiot. Did she flirt with everybody? He blinked and saw her frowning at him.

'You're not jealous of Tyson? Are you?'

Her voice sank in. Jake loosened his jaw with an effort.

'That was my ex-husband, Jake. He's someone else's problem now.'

Her ex-husband! He filled his lungs, feeling as if Poppy had pulled him out from under a pallet of bricks.

'One question. What were you doing, flirting with him in the corridor?'

'I wasn't flirting—I was poking him. The jerk asked me out.'

He watched that smile he loved sweep her features, and it felt good when she placed her hands on either side of his face. She was off balance against him, standing on tiptoe, and she felt gorgeously soft against his body. Actually, he wished she would burrow in.

'When you asked me out for dinner, the answer was different from the one I tried to sink into Tyson Harvey's thick brain. And I didn't flirt with him.' She frowned and screwed up her nose at the thought. 'Yuck.'

She was teasing him and it was driving him crazy. He had to get out of there. 'Well, don't forget our date. I'll see you tomorrow.'

The next evening, Jake rang Poppy's doorbell exactly at seven. He was raising his hand to his throat as if searching for a tie as she opened the door, and Poppy smiled to herself.

'You look gorgeous.' Jake's voice came out deeper than normal.

'Come in, Jake. I'm ready, but I need to lock the back door.' She felt the skirt of the dress swish around her as she turned away. The long, iridescent blue dress with bold red flowers fell from her cleavage to the floor. It seemed to mould and then release her curves in an intoxicating ritual.

'How do those tiny straps hold it all up?' His musing comment made her smile, and Poppy had that sixteen-year-old feeling again. Skittish and excited. Her skin felt tingly and the silly grin on her face had been there all afternoon.

'I've had a wonderful time, pampering myself for tonight, and I love your white shirt.' Actually, when she'd seen him standing outside her door, her heart had almost jumped out of her throat in response to the way the shirt emphasised the strong column of his throat.

When Poppy returned to the hallway Jake was standing where she had left him, a half-smile curving his sensual lips.

'Let's get out of here, Poppy. Or I won't be responsible for my actions.'

Her cheeks warmed. 'We could always stay home and eat cornflakes.'

'Out, woman. I need sustenance for the night ahead.' He teased her but his eyes were soft. 'Ah, Poppy, I can't wait to see you on the beach in the moonlight.'

He hugged her gently to him and she savoured the scent of his skin and the citrusy smell of his aftershave. Their lips met instinctively, as if they'd known each other for years, and Poppy sighed blissfully against his mouth. Her arms entwined themselves around his neck and her nipples hardened against his chest, the barrier of their clothing only teasing her more.

The kiss deepened and Poppy forgot the restaurant, the beach and everything else except this man and this moment.

His hands slid firmly, slowly, under her arms and down the sides of her body to her hips. When he reversed the caress, he pinched the fabric of her dress between his fingers and slid it up a few inches before stopping. He lifted his mouth away from hers.

'Does this material crush?'

Poppy, still dazed, had to think for a moment. 'No.' She pulled his mouth back to hers, to drink his breath into her soul.

His hands resumed their travelling up the sides of her body and the fabric of her dress bunched up over his wrists to expose her limbs and the white high-cut panties she wore. Now his hands were under her dress, his thumbs stroking across her flat stomach and his fingers wrapped around her towards her spine. Poppy shuddered with the sensation of his strong hands circling her, skin tingling on skin, completely within his power and yet more safe than she had ever felt before.

He lifted her slowly and as their lips parted his mouth trailed down her chin, along the offering of her arched throat and settled, for several heartbeats, below. She could feel his breath warming her skin as he breathed in and out. Then he lowered her again and hugged her to him. Every nerve in her being screamed out for her to lead him into her bedroom. To make him take her there, quickly and strongly, until they fused into one. She read the struggle in his eyes and they both smiled at the almost crackling air around them.

When they stepped apart neither said a word but, by mutual unspoken consent, decided not to rush things. Jake made her feel like a Dresden doll and it was addictive. Tyson had made her feel big and clumsy. Poppy picked up her tiny knitted bag and they stepped out into the night. This was getting really complicated.

Their table at the restaurant was against the window and screened from the only other couple by a shiny-leafed rubber tree. Jake was smiling indulgently at her and Poppy hadn't felt so desirable and pampered in years.

'Would you like a half-bottle of Chablis with your seafood, Poppy?'

She held up her hand hurriedly. 'No thanks, the champagne cocktail was lovely, but…' She slowed her voice down and spoke seductively out the side of her mouth. 'I am feeling dangerously relaxed here, Jake.' She fluttered her eyelashes at him and was delighted when he laughed out loud.

The very pregnant waitress coming towards them gave Poppy a 'lucky you' look and Poppy smiled back.

'How are you keeping, Debbie? I'm surprised you're still working.'

'I hate staying home on my own, Poppy, but I'm nearly ready for a holiday.' She smiled at Jake. 'The baby's due in four weeks. Would you like a bottle of wine?'

'Two lemon juices, please.' Jake handed back the wine list and winked at the compact tummy poking out at him. 'You must get heavy to carry around.'

'You carry the baby beautifully, Deb.' Poppy enjoyed seeing her antenatal class mothers as they grew closer to their babies' birth, but she thought Debbie looked tired.

The waitress rubbed her back tellingly and waved

as she waddled over to give a bill to the other couple.

Jake reached across the table, picked up Poppy's hand and enfolded it.

Poppy loved the way her small hand disappeared in his.

Their eyes met and she asked a question she needed to know the answer to. 'Why did you get into medicine, Jake?' She rested her chin in her other hand and watched the play of emotions on his face. For once he was allowing his feelings to show. He stroked her hand absently and she tried not to get distracted by the sensations.

'My father was a Crown Street heart specialist before he retired, and my mother has always been heavily into supporting medical charity functions. As the elder son, it seemed natural to become a doctor, like Dad.'

'Why paediatrics, then, and not cardiac medicine?' She watched the angles of his face soften and she could see why he'd chosen paediatrics.

'I really like kids. At school I used to do work experience in the children's ward at the local hospital once a week on different days. But not when the surf was up.'

He grinned up at her and she felt the kick of awareness tingle down her arms. Nobody deserved to be that sexy. He would have been lethal to the little surfie chicks, with a surfboard under his arm and wearing boardshorts.

'I think you're a lot like the ocean—deep and a little bit dangerous.' He captured her eyes with his. 'I was impressed with the way you swam in that badge swim the other week. You should have seen your face when I said there was a race for adults.' He threw his head back and laughed aloud at the memory.

Poppy loved the way Jake laughed, deep and rumbly. It was infectious. She grinned back at him and nudged him under the table. 'Rat.'

They teased and flirted with each other all through the meal and Poppy couldn't remember when she had enjoyed herself more. She wanted to know more about him.

'How do you see your role in medicine, Jake?'

All softness in his face vanished. 'I'm there to make people well. I keep searching for the answer and I don't give up. Although you made me rethink with that little anencephalic baby. I could have squandered the tiny amount of quality time he had with his parents. You made me realise that sometimes I'm afraid to let people die when their time has come.'

He took a deep breath and she realised that he'd reached a calmness about James. 'I did that to my own brother. He was right. I wouldn't have allowed him quality time. He had to come to strangers to find that peace.' He slid his hand from hers and picked up his glass. 'I have to live with that failure, but I don't have to repeat it.'

Poppy watched his strong throat as he swallowed, and she ached for all the times he'd been hurt and those times to come when he couldn't cure someone. And it would often be a child, in his line of medicine. It couldn't be healthy to carry all that baggage around.

She felt like saying, The load must get awfully heavy sometimes, Jake, and telling him she realised how hard it must have been for him to make such an admission. But she knew he'd finished with the subject.

'So were you in the surf club before you came up here?' She didn't know why but as soon as the words were out of her mouth she knew it was a bad question.

'Not for the last five years. My wife didn't like the beach.'

His what? Her arm slipped and the glass of lemon juice she was drinking almost ended up in her lap. The words seemed to hang in the air and Poppy felt the blood drain from her face. Not Tyson all over again, with her in the role of the other woman. She felt sick. Well, what had she expected? Jake was staring out of the window at the moonlight on the beach, and she wanted to throw her plate at him.

'She died three years ago,' he went on. 'Her mother was a charity-queen friend of my mother's.'

Poppy felt the blood rush back into her cheeks. Lucky she hadn't thrown that plate. She brushed the droplets of lemon juice from the tablecloth and mentally cringed. Jake didn't deserve her mistrust. Tyson really had soured her for other men. She could see she wasn't ready to trust men yet.

Tonight she would savour the evening. Tomorrow she would do some serious thinking about what was fair to Jake and what was fair to her. Poor Jake. He had enough baggage to carry, without her hang-ups. She suddenly realised what the time frame meant.

'I'm sorry to hear that, Jake. It must have been

terrible to lose your brother and your wife in the same year.'

'I don't really want to talk about it if you don't mind.' His voice was so empty of expression that she winced.

'Thank you for telling me, Jake.' The mood at the table was way too heavy for dessert, not that she could have eaten any. She forced a smile.

'Do you know that when Tyson left me Sandy let a jar of fleas loose in his car?' She watched his eyebrows rise in surprise and the twitch of his lips as he tried not to laugh. It made her feel happy that she could lift his spirits with her chatter.

Jake leaned forward and took her hand again. 'It's not that I don't believe that your friends would do that for you—but where would she get a jar of fleas?'

She looked down at his hand stroking hers. 'Her ten-year-old son. I have a very friendly relationship with him. Anyway, he was tired of his flea circus and donated them.' She smiled at the memory. 'Every time we saw Tyson before he left he was scratching. It certainly livened the ward up.'

'Poppy?'

She looked up.

'Do you think you'll get married again?'

She winced at the thought and had her own turn at looking away out of the window. 'No.' The answer was emphatic. She turned back to him. 'But I could happily live lustfully with someone as long as I had my own place and space to come home to.'

'What about children? In your job, don't you get

mushy with all those babies and happy couples everywhere?'

'Do you get clucky in your job, Jake? You must see some gorgeous kids that you want to take home.'

He shrugged. 'The last couple of years I can honestly say I haven't thought about having children myself. I know my parents would like me to settle down. My father wants to arrange a member's ticket for the Sydney Cricket Ground for my son if I ever have one—I think it takes about twenty years to come through! I know my mother has been waiting for a granddaughter to give that huge glory box she wouldn't give to her two sons.' He squeezed her hand. 'But I asked you first.'

Poppy turned her face back to his and smiled softly. 'Of course I'd love to have a baby.' She grimaced. 'That was another thing I couldn't do right in my marriage. But, boy, am I glad now. I'd rather have one on my own than have Tyson as the father of my children.'

Jake frowned. 'You're not one of these women who think that a child doesn't need two parents? I can see this fatherless child growing up playing a Pan flute.' He couldn't hide his shudder.

'Come on, Jake. Of course two parents are better if their relationship works, but you're not going to tell me that a bad father is better than no father? There are just as many dysfunctional nuclear families as there are single-parent families.'

'I disagree. Children need two parents. They can't become balanced without two role models.'

Poppy tilted her head and smiled slowly. 'My mother was the only parent I knew. My father died in Vietnam before I was born. You have egg on your face, mister. I'm very balanced in an unbalanced way.'

He held up his hands in defence. 'How do you keep doing this to me? I came here with a hatred of alternative therapies and now I find myself defending them against a medical colleague. And I'm not sure why!' Jake pretended to glare at her.

'But I still don't like the idea of single parents being acceptable—a view I have always disagreed with for as long as I remember, so don't try and change my mind.' He shook his head at her. 'Enough brainwashing for tonight, woman. You keep shooting down my long-held beliefs. What would you like for dessert?'

'Can we have ice-cream cones later and skip dessert now, please?'

'See what I mean? Dessert is the reason a lot of people eat out. It's where you can see how many ways the chef can disguise a mouthful of chocolate and strawberry.' He pursed his lips as if this were an extremely weighty matter. 'Tedious, now that I think about it. I'd love an ice cream later.'

She poked her tongue out at him from behind her hand, and his eyes darkened. Her stomach kicked at the flare of desire in his eyes but then it was gone and he was speaking as if it had never been.

'Being the conservative, white-collar individual that I am, I'll refrain from returning that salute. Let's get out of here.' He rose and moved to pull her chair out.

The balmy air met them as they left the restaurant and the sound of crashing waves tumbled in the background. Poppy's bag and shoes were stowed in the car boot and they strolled arm in arm down to the beach. The stars were shining and the waves tumbled from a dark mass to frothing white foam in the moonlight.

Poppy sighed and leaned into Jake's solid shoulder. The sand was still warm from the heat of the day's sun, and she wriggled her toes in delight. She looked at Jake's feet encased in expensive leather, and inwardly shrugged. She knew they were different.

'I've never seen beaches so deserted.' Jake stopped and slowly pulled Poppy around in a complete circle so they could see there were no other people on the beach.

'You're just a city boy. Beaches are supposed to be private places.'

Jake smiled into her face. 'I'm very partial to private places.' He pulled her against him and she snuggled into his arms.

'I think you're getting a one-track mind. I was wondering if it's on the same track as mine?' She tilted her face, inviting his kiss, something she had craved more than anything all evening.

He stared into her eyes and the sound of the waves on the beach receded, and the new waves of anticipation rippled through her body like an incoming set. Each ripple was larger than the last until her feet were swept from under her and the whisper of Jake breathing her name was like a lighthouse in the storm as his lips met hers.

They closed their eyes. Two bodies, two hearts

and one long, searing embrace that fuelled their hunger until it swirled them into a sea of passion.

'Poppy!'

A man's strident voice shattered the moment into a million pieces of might-have-beens. Poppy and Jake stepped apart and stared at the man jogging breathlessly towards them. It was Daniel—Debbie's husband—from the restaurant.

CHAPTER SEVEN

'THANK goodness I found you. It's Debbie. Her waters have broken. I know it's supposed to take hours, but I think the baby is coming now.'

Jake spoke first. 'Have you phoned for the ambulance? Debbie said she had four weeks to go and her dates could be wrong. She could be earlier. We'd want suction and oxygen and emergency drugs just in case.'

Daniel looked even more worried and glanced at Poppy. 'Not yet. I thought I'd wait for Poppy to see what she reckons.'

Jake frowned and Poppy laid her hand on his arm. 'Phone now, Daniel. Everything will be fine. Dr Sheppard and I will be right behind you.'

Daniel turned and ran for the restaurant. Jake and Poppy didn't speak as they jogged after him. Poppy was busy with her own thoughts. She hoped Jake wasn't going to keep predicting the worst. She cleared the frown from her face. That wasn't fair. At the hospital people looked to Jake when things didn't go to plan. She couldn't blame him for anticipating difficulties and wanting to be prepared.

The curtains were drawn in the restaurant but the door was open. Debbie was leaning up against the cocktail bar. Her knuckles were white where she gripped the brass rail and her knees were slightly bent. Her hips were swaying from side to side while she breathed through the contraction, and she sighed limply as the pain receded. She looked up with relief as Poppy walked across to stand beside her.

'Hello, Deb. You're doing beautifully there. I heard that lovely big sigh after the pain finished.' Poppy's voice was very quiet and matter-of-fact. 'Remember to have one at the beginning as well.'

Poppy gently massaged the girl's shoulders until the tautness drained away. 'So, tell me, what are you feeling in the middle of the contraction?'

'Pressure.' Debbie ducked her head in embarrassment. 'Like I urgently have to go to the toilet. Is the baby too young to be born, Poppy?'

Poppy smiled wryly and patted her on the shoulder. 'Worry and labour don't go together. OK, remember your classes, woman,' she teased.

'I'm glad you're here, Poppy.' She smiled tremulously at Poppy who smiled back.

'Your baby is about two to four weeks early. If he or she were to have any problem, it would usually happen later. A lot of babies born this early have no problems at all. You're also very privileged, because tonight I chose to come to dinner with a paediatrician who likes nothing better than meeting new little babies.'

'Life is always interesting with Poppy around,' Jake said, and she saw him offer his own reassuring smile.

Poppy relaxed at Jake's compliance. She'd been worried he would want to heave Debbie into a car and roar off to hospital. Not a bad idea if she hadn't been almost in second stage. Poppy really didn't want to have the baby born at the side of the road.

The ambulance could make it here from Midcoast at best in twenty minutes, and then at least the baby could be born in warmth.

'Maybe you'll both have to stay in hospital longer than you would have, but by the time your baby's due date arrives you'll both be home again, probably a lot earlier, though,' Poppy said.

She watched the girl frown and breathe deeply as another contraction gripped her. Poppy stood behind her with her hands on Debbie's hips and they swayed and breathed together through the contraction. She felt Debbie catch her breath and involuntarily give a bearing-down push. There was no need to guess what was going to happen soon.

Daniel was back and sweating. Poppy swapped places with him. 'Support her weight when she wants you to. Remember this is a special time and don't be frightened. You're both doing great. Jake and I are going to get some things together so we'll poke around in your kitchen, all right?'

Poppy saw Daniel give her a don't-leave-me look and she rested her hand on his shoulder for a minute. 'Back in one moment. The next pain won't be here for two minutes.' She grinned and Daniel whistled air through his teeth in relief.

Jake followed Poppy into the kitchen. 'Don't you have to examine her to tell if she's going to have the baby soon?'

Poppy smiled gently at him. 'Nope. She's going to have her baby very soon. Her body told her so and even mentioned it to me. Come on, let's find some gear.'

Stainless steel shone everywhere and Poppy

opened the door of the dishwasher, stepping back quickly as the steam from the drying cycle billowed past her cheek. She left that for a moment and went through some drawers until she came up with a neat stack of white tea towels.

She spread one out on the bench as if this were a normal day in the central sterilising department and chose her instruments from the dishwasher with two tea towels wrapped around her hands. Jake stood and waited for instructions.

'This is your show, I can tell.' He shook his head again. 'Amazing woman.'

She chose a steel salad bowl, 'It's Debbie's show and all women are amazing.' She winked at him. She turned back to the choices in front of her.

'For the placenta,' she muttered, lifting a pair of kitchen scissors. 'We could always not cut the cord,' she mused to herself, and wrapped the scissors in a separate towel inside the bundle. She looked up at Jake.

'Boil the jug and find me something to tie the cord with, please, Jake. We'll sterilise whatever we tie it with in the water, but I'm hoping the ambulance will bring me some cord clamps in time to make it easier. I've got a wonderful emergency set at home—a lot of good that will do me.' She shrugged. 'But we'll manage.'

She scrubbed her hands and wrists at the sink and laughed out loud as she bundled up her 'instruments'. 'Not a bad place to find what you need to have a baby.'

Debbie had just started the next pain when Poppy patted Daniel on the shoulder. He looked up with a strained smile of welcome and Poppy encouraged him with a gesture to stay where he was.

She didn't want to talk while Debbie was concentrating on her body's messages, and she noted how the pushing was becoming more forceful. Poppy lifted her own long skirt up to her thighs and tied a knot in it to keep the hem out of her way. Finally the contraction was finished and Deb sagged against her husband in relief.

'Can you get Deb a glass of iced water, please, Daniel, while we attend to some clothing adjustments?' Daniel stepped around Poppy and slid behind the bar. Poppy laughed at the sound of ice being poured into a glass.

'We need a cocktail bar in the birthing unit. That's great service.' She helped Deb remove her bra from under her shirt, as well as her underpants and skirt, before the next contraction interrupted them. They stood and while the pain lasted swayed together on a little circle of tea towels Poppy had placed under them.

Jake appeared at Poppy's shoulder and she looked up. 'Oh, good. I've a job for you. Can you make a bed with these cushions on the floor, please? Even if we only use it after the baby is born.' She turned to Deb. 'Do you want to have baby standing at the rail or do you want to squat or lie down, Deb?'

'I don't know,' wailed Deb, and Poppy hid a smile.

Too many options. Poppy pulled the girl against her chest and cuddled her for a moment. Deb looked up with damp eyes and smiled tremulously at Poppy.

'It's pretty scary, isn't it, Poppy?'

'You're doing a fabulous job.' She gestured to the worried father. 'Daniel, can you sit down here on the lounge then Deb can lean her back between your knees and you can support her under the arms? That way she's in a supported squat and can see what's going on.'

Debbie looked a bit uncertain about that. Poppy smiled when she caught the look.

'It's all right. Close your eyes if you want to. We'll move you if you don't like it. But I think it's all going to happen pretty soon anyway.' She helped Debbie to position herself in front of her husband, and set her 'instruments' out on a tea towel on the floor in front of them. Jake handed her a small steel bowl with several long pieces of string lying damply in the bottom.

The next contraction started and Debbie moaned as her face screwed up in concentrated pushing. The first downy crown of the baby's head could be seen bulging between Debbie's legs, and the room was quiet except for the sounds of nature bringing a new life into the world.

Poppy soaked in the magic of the moment as she quietly encouraged Debbie to gently push the baby's head out of the birth canal. The baby's face swept the perineum and the head squeezed through the opening in his mother's body. Debbie groaned with the effort and Poppy soothed her with praise.

'Wonderful, Debbie. Baby has a crick in his neck at the moment and soon Baby's head will turn a little as the shoulders rotate through your pelvis. When that happens, Baby will slide out. Feel the head there.' She took Debbie's hand and lowered it to stroke the wet hair of her child.

'Oh, wow. My baby. Our baby.' Debbie leaned her head back against her husband's chest, and Daniel dropped a fervent kiss on his wife's cheek.

'Oh,' Debbie whimpered. 'The baby's head is moving.' The little head swivelled in a half-circle and then stopped. Poppy supported the infant's cheeks with both of her hands so that first one shoulder and then the other came out from under the pelvic bone. Then the baby slid wetly into the world to lie on the towels in front of his parents.

Jake wiped the tiny boy's face with a tea towel and rubbed his little chest. The baby spluttered and mewed at the irritation, then bellowed his displeasure.

Daniel stared with tears running down his cheeks and Debbie was laughing exultantly after the effort. She pulled off her shirt to bare her skin as if it was the most natural thing in the world. Poppy encouraged her to reach down and lift the baby carefully up to her chest, skin to skin. The cord was long, and dangled, pulsating and shiny purple, against her skin. Poppy tucked a tea towel around the baby to keep in the warmth.

Poppy's eyes met Jake's and she swallowed the lump in her throat as she smiled. She watched the strong column of his throat as he swallowed, too. He tilted his head in congratulation and she knew it was a moment both of them would never forget.

The sound of an approaching ambulance siren interrupted the scene. Poppy frowned, and spent the next fifteen minutes trying to keep the transfer of mother and baby as free from disruption as possible. She even had the ambulance officers tiptoeing around the room. Jake stood and watched it all and she saw his shoulders shaking with suppressed laughter.

Driving home in the car later, Poppy was aware of a new closeness between them.

'You're a special person, Poppy. You do a terrific job. I'm really starting to see what you offer your labouring mums. You make people feel good and able to deal with situations to the best of their ability. It's a very special gift and totally different to the way I was taught to think of medicine.'

'Thank you, Jake. That's the nicest compliment I've ever had.'

He slanted a look at her and she could see his teeth shine in the dark as they pulled up outside her house.

'Well, if that's the best, these country boys must be less talkative than even I thought they were.'

When he followed her inside, it was natural to turn into his arms and raise her face.

He captured her mouth then lifted her effortlessly into his arms and carried her through to the bedroom, before returning her feet to the floor. He made her feel so dainty and feminine. She had to admit it felt wonderful to be in the arms of a strong man. She stood, protected in the circle of his embrace, and rested her forehead against the hard wall of his chest.

There was no rush. The night was young, filled with promise and new life in more ways than one.

Poppy stepped to the window and opened the curtains to allow the moonlight to fall on the bed, before returning to stand in front of him. Still there was silence as they communicated with their eyes.

She crossed her hands in front of her knees and slowly pulled the dress over her head until she stood semi-naked and sensually silver in the moonlight.

She heard the hiss of Jake's indrawn breath and exulted in his response. This man made her feel more powerfully feminine than she had ever imagined she could. As if in a mutual dance, he slowly crossed his hands at his waist and drew his own shirt up and over his head, and the moonlight turned him into a silver statue.

It was her turn to breathe deeply as the planes of his muscular chest rippled and expanded with the movement, igniting a response deep in her stomach that kindled the smouldering flames of desire into sudden heat. He kicked off his shoes, flipped open his belt and slid his trousers and briefs off in one fluid movement. Then he stood before her, gloriously naked.

He seemed larger than life, potently masculine and an awesome sight in the moonlight.

Poppy matched him, straightening her back before sinuously sliding her white lace pants down her thighs and lower legs until she stepped delicately out of them. She refused to allow herself to be overawed, and made the first move.

Poppy crossed the floor to brush her proud nipples and breasts against Jake's chest in a languid indulgence of sensation. She closed her eyes and savoured the roughness of his chest hairs against her own soft skin and shuddered with a sensation that, despite its simplicity, was erotically beautiful. She felt the moisture of tears sting her eyes and was strangely empowered by their mutual restraint.

He left her side for a moment, and the rustle of foil tearing made her smile. This time he was prepared.

When he returned she shivered in anticipation as his strong hands clasped her shoulders, before sliding down her body until they rested at her waist. He spanned her waist as he had earlier in the evening, except this time there was no barrier of clothing between them.

It was time to lie together and discover old secrets and new as he lifted her into his arms to lay her before him on the bed. Then she was lost in the shifting skin tones shining in the moonlight. The beams drifted further across the bed with the setting of the moon, settling on the dozing couple, their arms and legs entwined in sleep or caressing in movement, before disappearing with the early morning light.

CHAPTER EIGHT

POPPY was pregnant. She gently put the phone down after thanking her friend in the pathology department. A positive beta HcG blood test. It must have happened that first time, as they'd been more sensible since then. She crossed her arms over her stomach, careful not to touch her tender breasts. Jake's baby!

A hundred thoughts crowded her mind and she didn't know whether to laugh or cry.

A baby!

She had wanted a child for so long but what would Jake say? This child would create a tie with a man who stood for everything she'd sworn she would avoid in any future relationship. Someone she didn't even fully trust. Though, to be fair, he hadn't let her down. Yet.

But he was handsome, conservative and still a bit of a stuffed shirt as far as alternative therapies went. Just like her ex-husband. She wasn't going down that road again. From the little he'd told her about his parents, they were as far removed from her mother the hippy as they could possibly be. Poppy winced. Her child's grandparents.

She and Jake didn't have any ties to each other. But they were having a child. She picked up the phone and dialled his number then put it down again, needing time to get used to the idea. She stared at the palm tree outside the window. Maybe she'd go back to Dorrigo. It would be worth it for the sense of peace that never failed her in the rain-forest. She'd ring Jake when she got home.

Although tired and physically aching from the forest walk, Poppy was mentally rested. She wanted Jake's baby more than anything in the world, and was sure she would be a good mother. However, she wasn't sure how Jake was going to feel, but she could make it on her own anyway.

Poppy looked at the phone again. She knew Jake was conventional. His parents were conventional. She hoped he wouldn't be worried about the stigma of illegitimacy. Anyway, she'd sleep on it tonight and tell him tomorrow.

When Poppy went to work the next day, Tyson was the first person she saw.

'So your boyfriend had to go away.' He was smirking and she narrowed her eyes at him.

'Get out of my face, Tyson. Jake's a friend, not my boyfriend.' She turned her back on him. 'But if he had to go away he would have told me himself.' Her voice sounded small, even to her.

'Ho, ho! Poor Poppy. So he didn't give you a kiss goodbye.' He walked around in front of her again. 'Looks like you're stuck with just me for the next few weeks.'

Poppy looked him up and down and laughed mirthlessly. 'Oh, I'm cured of you. I've got work to do. Excuse me.' She pushed past him and went to look for Sandy. Why hadn't Jake told her he was going away?

When she found Sandy, washing bowls, her friend's sympathy was just as hard to bear as Tyson's innuendoes had been. His father had a heart attack early yesterday afternoon, Sandy said quietly. 'Apparently he drove down there straight away. Are you sure he didn't leave you a message?'

'I was out. I had some thinking to do. I need to talk to Jake.' Poppy felt like wringing her hands.

'What do you need to talk to him about, or is that a personal question?'

Poppy smiled weakly. 'Since when would that stop you?' She looked up at her friend. 'I'm pregnant.'

'Oh, no!' Sandy slumped back against the pan-room wall. 'Haven't you two heard about birth control?'

Poppy chewed her lip. 'It was an accident.'

'I should bloody well hope so.' Sandy frowned and looked Poppy in the eye. 'You've only known him two months. What did he say? Are you going to marry him?'

'He doesn't know and he hasn't asked me.' She avoided her friend's eyes. 'But there's no way I'm marrying anybody. Jake would probably have some involvement as the baby's father, although when we talked about children he said he didn't want a baby himself. Just for his parents.' Sandy's brows were climbing higher but she didn't say anything.

Poppy went on less confidently, 'I hope he'll stay in Midcoast to be near his child. But, either way, I've my own house, I can support a child and still do the work I love with fewer shifts.' Her voice was starting to sound even less sure. 'I thought you'd be happy for me.'

Sandy tilted her head at her friend. 'Oh, I'm happy. Congratulations.' She reached into her pocket to pull out a butterscotch. 'Here. Have a sweet.' She snorted. 'Why do I get the feeling you'd be quite happy if Jake never came back and you could ride off into the sunset with your baby?'

'That's a horrible thing to say. I can't believe you're saying this.'

'I love you, Poppy, but I've seen the walls you can build if you feel threatened in your safe ways. Don't be afraid to get close to him.' She looked up and smiled gently at her friend. 'Obviously you've been close at least once—open your heart to him, too. Jake's a little domineering, but he's trustworthy. I think you should trust him to do what's right for you and the child you're *both* having.'

Sandy pushed herself off the wall and patted Poppy on the shoulder. 'He may not be happy with the neat little visiting rights you've worked out for him either.'

Jake was away for three weeks. Even though Poppy had spoken to him often on the phone, there had never seemed to be a right time to share the news. She was starting to regret not having rung him as soon as she'd found out. Every time she saw Sandy at work she was haunted by their conversation.

The night Jake came back it was even harder to come to the point. She'd invited Jake over for dinner to welcome him home. The table was set and they were sitting, relaxed, in the lounge room—or at least Jake was.

Poppy licked dry lips and hovered between determination to tell him and nausea. The nausea probably had about fifty per cent to do with the morning sickness that had been getting worse every day for the last week, and the rest was nerves.

'Jake?'

'Hmm?'

'Look at me.' She watched him lift his eyes to her face, and the gentle expression on his face gave her strength.

She took a deep breath. 'I'm having a baby. Our baby.'

His eyebrows snapped together and she could almost hear his mind whirring as he stared at her. He stood up and turned his back on her. Damn. She wanted to see the expressions cross his face. Would he look surprised, rueful, serious, determined, happy—what? She clenched her hands together.

'When did you find out?' He kept his back to her.

'The day before you went to Sydney.' She looked at the dark hair curling just above his collar. 'Jake? Say something.'

'What do you want me to say, Poppy?' He turned back to her. His face was guarded.

'I wanted to see your face.'

'Did anyone see your face when you found out?' Poppy winced at his tone but admitted he had a point. She'd gone away for the day so she could think it through. It seemed so long ago now.

'I'll bet they didn't.' He sounded cynical and she glimpsed what looked like fear in his eyes.

She felt her throat close over. Did he think she was going to try to trap him? Want him to marry her? A little voice inside her head whispered that he didn't fancy that at all—which shouldn't have hurt after what she'd already decided—but it did.

Her voice was tentative. 'The baby is due in the middle of July. I'd like you to be with me when he or she is born.'

Now he looked offended. 'Of course I'll be with you. I would assume I would be with my wife when she's giving birth to *our* baby.' Duty called. This was what she'd been afraid of.

'Was that a proposal, Jake?' She spoke gently and watched his gaze refocus on her. He looked like a child caught with his hand in the biscuit jar.

'Sorry, Poppy.' He sat down beside her on the lounge and took her hand in his. 'Will you do me the honour of being my wife?'

She felt her eyes mist. He was such a decent man. He was even pretending the idea wasn't the last thing he wanted. The nausea came out of nowhere. She clapped her hand over her mouth and stumbled to the toilet, waving him away with her hand so that he didn't follow her, then pulling the door shut behind her.

Jake stared after her. Well, that was a different response to a proposal. Hell. He remembered her saying she wouldn't get married again, but shrugged. That wouldn't apply to this situation. He was really fond of Poppy but he would have liked to have felt less locked out when he was with her before making such a commitment. Sometimes she was incredibly open and at others it was as if she were on one side of the Katherine Gorge and he on the other. But it had happened.

He grinned to himself. His mother would have a fit. She'd say they had to get married before Poppy started to show and pronounce the child premature. God love her. Wait till she met Poppy.

He walked around the room. A child. His child. The thought made him remember feelings he didn't want to resurrect.

He'd already had a child—one that had died because he hadn't been there with its mother. Even though everyone said it hadn't been his fault, he should have realised that her asthma had worsened as the pregnancy had progressed. The final attack had happened while he'd been away overnight at a conference.

A chilling thought froze his darting mind. What if something happened to Poppy or the baby? He didn't want to think about it. It was too late now to fear commitment.

When Poppy came back into the room, she felt what little colour she had drain from her face. Jake's expression held all the fear and dismay she'd prayed he wouldn't feel. It was her fault. He looked like a man facing the gallows. Well, what had she expected? A woman he'd only known for a few months was having his baby. And he felt he had to marry her.

She wanted to reassure him, but a black fist seemed to close around her heart as she acknowledged that, despite all her brave plans, one part of her was deeply disappointed at his response. Pull yourself together, woman. You've decided on a course of action—all you have to do is go through with it.

He looked up and saw her, then laid his arm across her shoulders. 'Are you OK?' He ran a finger beneath her hairline, a fleeting touch she felt right down her spine. She nodded.

'So is this a bad time to ask you again?'

She stroked his handsome face. 'Jake, I want you to listen to me.' She watched him nod and forced herself to go on. 'I can't marry you.' His mouth opened to protest but she touched his lips with her finger. 'Listen.'

'I enjoy the time I spend with you. I didn't plan this pregnancy but I'm thrilled about it. I want to be a mother. If I wanted to be married, I'm sure you would be the best husband. But that's it. I don't want to be a wife. Not even your wife.' She watched his face harden as her words penetrated. He lifted his arm off her shoulder and contrarily she wanted it back.

'So where does that leave me?'

She could see the effort he was making to stay reasonable, and it hurt her that she had to do this to him. But there was no way she was travelling down that road again. Even worse, this time the man would marry her because of an illegitimate baby. Second-class citizen all over again. No way. She was fighting for her self-respect here.

'It leaves you as the father of our child, with as much or as little involvement as you want.'

He started to pace the tiny lounge room. The energy from his body crowded the small room and Poppy closed her eyes to shut out the sight of him.

He stopped moving and she opened her eyes. He was in front of her.

'Gee, thanks. Get real, Poppy.' He shot her a scathing look. 'I want to see your belly grow and feel my child move in the womb. I don't want to be a part-time father with visiting rights. I want to be there when he wakes you up in the middle of the night and you soothe him with your breast. I want to hear his first word and see his first step. You shouldn't want to take that away from me.' He stopped and loomed over her. 'Why do you?'

'I don't want to take that from you, Jake. I think it sounds wonderful. We could spend a lot of time together, but I'm not marrying you. And I'm not giving up my home.'

'Fine. I'll live here when the baby's born. Hell, I might move in straight away. Get used to me, Poppy. I may not have a piece of paper to say we're married but that's how it's going to feel.' His expression dared her to object and she couldn't say anything. She sat with her mouth open and stared at this madman in her lounge room.

'I'm going for a drive. I'll be back.' He glared at her and grabbed his keys off the hallstand. The sound as his car started drifted in through the open front door and Poppy sighed.

Men. If she didn't feel so sick she'd throw him out when he came back. Then she decided she couldn't be bothered so she took the key out from under the frog inside with her and locked the door instead. Then she went to bed.

Jake didn't move into Poppy's house but he might as well have. He started to bring groceries and cook meals that Poppy didn't eat until she was just over sixteen weeks pregnant. Christmas and New Year passed in a blur. Jake bought her a tiny nativity-scene music box and that was her only festive decoration. He'd wanted to put up a tree but she wouldn't let him as it seemed too much of a commitment to dress a tree together. And she was too sick.

She dragged herself to work and made the effort to be cheerful and efficient for her clients, but by the time she made it home after her shift she couldn't do anything but lie on the bed feeling miserably unwell.

Jake had tried to reason with her to give up work or at least take her annual holidays, but Poppy wanted no extra bills left by the time the baby was born.

Towards the end of February the morning, afternoon and evening sickness finally eased off—a month after it was supposed to—and Poppy surfaced to find Jake ensconced in her daily routines.

She watched his long fingers rhythmically peel the skin from the potatoes at the sink and felt a slow swirling of desire twist its way through her stomach. It was the first libidinous thought she'd had in months. The potato was round and skin-coloured and he almost caressed it as he worked.

She watched the ripples in his shoulders as his arms moved, and the swirls became whirlpools as she drank in the sight of him. Her tongue moistened dry lips. They hadn't made love since Debbie had had her baby.

'Jake?'

'Hmm?' He didn't look up but stopped the cheerful accompaniment to the radio song he was singing as he puttered around the kitchen.

'Why don't you stay the night sometimes?'

He looked up at her from under his brows, then shook his head. 'Tut-tut. Are you trying to seduce me?' He looked innocently at her.

'Could I?' She glanced down at her rounded abdomen and too thin arms and legs. His face softened. It made the ever-present tears prick her eyes and she scrubbed them away impatiently with her fingers.

'You could seduce me with the tip of your little finger, lady, but you've been so sick. I've gone home and lived in the cold shower for the last two months.' He dried his hands on the towel and crossed the room to her. He folded her into his arms and hugged her gently against him. His eyes were twinkling. 'Are you feeling better, Ms McCrae?'

'I think I might live. Yes.' She twisted her hands up around his neck and pulled his face down to hers. 'Please, kiss me so I know I'm alive.'

'I can't believe it. She's back!'

Jake stayed the night and by morning Poppy knew that she was definitely alive. It was Saturday and Jake was off duty. But not off kitchen duty.

'Wake up, Sleeping Beauty. Happy Valentine's Day.' Jake's voice drifted over her and she couldn't help the satisfied smile on her face as memories of the night before surfaced, along with her sense of smell. Warm croissants. She opened her eyes to see a smiling Jake holding a breakfast tray. She sat up in the bed and blew him a kiss for the single red rose on the tray.

Her forehead creased. 'Wasn't Valentine's Day last week?'

He grinned. 'True, Miss Pedantic, but you were too sick last week, so I thought today seemed a better day for it.'

'Why Dr Sheppard, you're a romantic! I could get used to this,' she said without thinking, and then looked away. She was the one holding back, not him. She was the one worried about what happened when the honeymoon was over.

'My sentiments exactly. Now, Ms McCrae, do you fancy a croissant or would you like plain toast?'

'I would like you to stop calling me Ms McCrae.' Why was she suddenly feeling pettish? Maybe his cheerfulness was getting to her.

'That is what we're going to talk about later, but for now decide what you want to eat and I'll leave you to recover your good humour.' Jake stood beside her bed patiently, and Poppy wanted to throw a pillow at him.

'Croissant and tea, thanks,' she muttered.

He bowed mock-subserviently, and as he backed out the door she thought she heard him say, 'Such graciousness.' It made her smile at herself and her moods. Jake really was wonderful. She shifted uneasily in the bed. What did he want to talk about?

Jake didn't know how to convince her. The last eight weeks of just being with Poppy had been some of the most satisfying he could remember. It certainly hadn't been exciting, but he'd been there.

Even the wind chimes had become a pleasant accompaniment to natural sounds. He realised now that the feelings he held for Poppy would only get stronger.

Even miserably unwell, she captivated and brought out the best in him. Although he wasn't sure if he brought out the best in her. He grinned. Pregnancy made for interesting moods. He couldn't imagine not being in her life and the life of his unborn child. He wanted to protect her from the world and share his life with her. But she wouldn't let him in because she still didn't trust him.

'Poppy, this pushing yourself so hard at work has to stop.' They were sitting on the back verandah overlooking the river that afternoon when Jake launched his campaign. 'Let me help with expenses. I was half the reason you aren't really well enough to work.'

'No, Jake. I'm fine. You already do enough. You pay for food and you don't even live here.'

He winked. 'That could be arranged.'

'No, Jake. Thanks but, no, thanks.'

Jake clenched his teeth behind his smile, trying not to let Poppy see how frustrated he was becoming. 'Poppy, I want to marry you and settle down. Make a commitment to you and our child. You're not being fair to me.'

Poppy cringed. *You're not being fair to me!* Tyson had said that when she hadn't performed up to his standards—worn the wrong dress, not had an elaborate enough meal, spent an evening with her mother. And Jake hadn't mentioned love.

Poppy almost cried. Was it her? Was she destined to make the men in her life feel they were getting ripped off? Couldn't Jake see that their relationship would be more stable—not less—if they didn't get married? The tears hovered at the back of her eyes. She couldn't cope with this now—she seemed to have spent half her time crying this last month. She had to have some space. This was exactly why she didn't want to get married.

'Jake, I'm feeling much better today. I really appreciate your help. You've been wonderful for the last eight weeks but I'm over the worst of it now. You have your own life and I have mine. I think I need some space.'

'So that's it, is it?' He glared at her but she could see the pain in his eyes. He stood up and towered over her. 'You don't need me any more so I'm dismissed.' He turned away and then wheeled back again. 'Thanks for the night in bed. Hell. You probably didn't need me after conception. Did you, Poppy?'

She sucked in her breath. How dared he? She felt her heart shrivel in hurt and blinked back the tears. Damn him. When she spoke her voice was very quiet.

'Get out of my house!'

She rose out of the chair, turned her back on him, walked into the house and her room and shut the door quietly behind her.

She leaned her back against it, drawing shallow breaths as the tears streamed down her face. Damn him. The most painful part about it was the element of truth in his statement. She'd laughed about a sperm donor with her sister before she'd even slept with Jake. What did that make her? So much for keeping her self-respect intact.

She swallowed, trying to clear the lump in her throat and ease the tightness in her chest. It was harder to catch her breath and she could hear a wheeze. She pushed herself off the door to rummage in the bedside table for her Ventolin puffer.

After several minutes she began to breathe more easily and sat in the bedroom chair until the tightness had gone. She'd better sign up for that breathing course if her asthma was going to play up in pregnancy. She hated taking Ventolin. She scowled.

Jake was livid. With himself. He'd seen the hurt he'd caused. He knew her history with the jerk that had ground the self-respect out of her. Cassandra had filled him in when he'd asked. What right did he have to do the same? He loved Poppy. He could admit that now that he'd blown it. He'd been too impatient. Too stupid. Jake smacked himself on the forehead. Jerk.

'OK.' He spoke to the rear-view mirror as he drove home. 'Start again. Back off for a while then woo her.' He was that crazy for her that he didn't care if he had to listen to Pan flutes for the rest of his life. His face softened. The way they'd made love last night she had to have feelings for him. He held onto that thought.

Jake didn't visit Poppy at her house for the next four weeks. To Poppy it felt like four years. They passed the time of day at work and she began to gain weight now that the nausea had passed. She missed his presence and surprise visits more than she'd thought she would. The first time she felt the baby move made Poppy realise how much she wanted to share the pregnancy with him.

She held the phone to her ear. 'Jake? It's Poppy.' He sounded sleepy and she cringed at the thought of waking him. She felt like an idiot for ringing.

'Poppy? What's wrong?' She could hear a tiny thread of panic in his voice and she frowned.

'Are you busy? It was stupid to ring you so late. It wasn't anything. I'll see you tomorrow.'

'Don't hang up.' His voice softened. 'Tell me, I want to know.'

Poppy's face warmed with embarrassment. 'I felt the baby kick for the first time. I've had flutters before but this was a real kick.'

'Wow.'

She heard the delight in his voice and relaxed. It was OK. He didn't think she was mad.

'That's all, Jake.' Her heart squeezed inside her. She missed him.

'Poppy. Thanks for ringing me. I miss you.'

Her eyes stung. She couldn't talk. Her throat closed over and she knew he would tell that she was crying. Swallowing frantically, she tried to make her voice work, but all she achieved was a croaky, 'Bye.' She clattered the phone back on the hook and sniffed. She was doing the right thing.

Over the next month they had a few laughs in passing at work, had a couple of Chinese meals and Jake had tea at Jasmine's house twice. He and the boys seemed to spend most of the time rolling on the ground with a football, and Poppy knew her sister thought she was mad not to marry Jake before he changed his mind.

Sometimes she thought she was mad, too. Towards the end of the month he started to drop around at her house when neither of them were working. Jake never mentioned marriage.

Poppy was six months pregnant and had to consciously stop herself from waddling when she walked. She was even starting to wonder if maybe he didn't want to marry her now.

Halfway through April, Poppy started her next group of Wednesday night antenatal classes. Jake offered to drive her in his car. She actually agreed and he felt as if he'd won a small victory.

'I'm really looking forward to these classes,' he commented. And it was a good excuse to spend more time with her.

'This is so weird. Being pregnant and running antenatal classes.' Poppy smiled at him and he squeezed her knee.

'You look great. I love that colour on you.' She looked gorgeous in a green and white polka-dot maternity dress, and he was having a hard time keeping his hands off her.

'I try to wear blue or turquoise on the first night.' She felt the material against her throat. 'Blue stimulates the throat chakra and helps with public speaking.'

Jake lifted his brows. 'How can a colour help?'

But he was mentally shaking his head and wondering what new bizarre idea she'd come up with. The funny thing was that it didn't seem to worry him any more. Maybe he was getting more open-minded in his old age.

'I still get a little nervous on the first night, and I find if I wear these colours it all seems to flow more smoothly. Different crystals and stones help with different things, and the same goes for colours. See?' She lifted her hair away from her ears and he glanced quickly at her earrings, before looking back at the road.

'So you wear turquoise earrings and it helps you speak well.' He bit back a grin but it was there in his voice. 'I'll have to remember to buy myself a blue shirt next time I need to get my point across.'

'Cynic.' He heard her draw a quick breath. 'Oh.' She put her hand over her stomach and smiled. She took his hand to feel, too.

He loved it when she lifted his palm to lay it over her stomach and feel the baby kick. She'd done it the night before as well. He'd been more at ease since he'd decided to be satisfied with what Poppy felt comfortable to give. He believed it would all work out in the end. It had to.

'The course runs for eight weeks and we cover a different topic each week.' Poppy handed around the outline of the course and she blushed when it was Jake's turn to receive one.

'Also, every week we'll do fifteen minutes of relaxation and visualisation, and you'll really benefit if you practise at home. Relaxation techniques are something you can carry with you for your whole life. Even after your baby is born and won't sleep when you want him to.' The class laughed and Poppy smiled as she tried to guess the ones who'd confidently assume that their children would sleep.

'If you take one thing home with you from the classes, I'd like you to remember this. Your body is quite capable of this remarkable achievement as long as you listen to the messages it gives you. You're designed to have babies.

'Now, don't feel left out, fellows, you were designed to put them there.' The class laughed and she blushed again when she caught Jake's eye. She moved on hurriedly.

'Think about the concept. The baby's head can change shape to fit through your pelvis, and your pelvis can stretch and bend to allow the baby through. Each contraction moves down in a wave-like fashion and makes the space that the baby's living in smaller. Therefore, the baby is propelled out through the pelvis.'

She looked around. 'Sound simple? Well, it is! But it's very hard work, staying calm and relaxed while your body does this. That's why you're attending classes—not for me to give you the answers, but so you can problem-solve your way through labour when the time comes.'

Katrina, a young single mum, had a notebook on her lap and had been earnestly writing down Poppy's words. 'How do you know when it's time? When to go to the hospital or if you're really in labour? My friend went into hospital too early and her labour stopped. She had to go home and everyone had already seen her car out in front of Maternity! She was really embarrassed.'

The class murmured at the thought and Poppy was glad the point had been brought up.

'For the first part of your question, we'll discuss all the signs of labour in more detail next week but, basically, it's time if your waters break or you have regular, painful contractions less than five minutes apart and you don't feel ''safe'' any more. Can anyone think of a good reason why God has arranged for a woman to feel pain as she goes into labour?'

Nobody answered and Poppy caught Jake's eye as he indicated that he had no idea. She raised her eyebrows and shook her head at him. And he was a doctor.

'Think about it.' There was silence and a few comments until one of the women called out, 'Because He's a man.' Poppy grinned at her.

'More likely because She's a woman. It's a perfect way to make you stop what you're doing and look for somewhere safe to prepare for your baby's arrival.

'Which brings us to the second part of the question—when to come into hospital. Remember that for your labour to progress you need to be comfortable and relaxed in your surroundings. Human beings are the only animals who make a lovely nest and desert it at the last minute to have their babies.'

Jake started to cough and she could see he was struggling to keep from smiling. She remembered the first night she'd met him, and his disagreement with this comment. Squeezing her own lips together, she looked away before she lost her train of thought. She'd get him later.

'If your body doesn't feel safe to allow itself to progress in labour then it will stop. Sometimes the initial nervousness you feel as you go into hospital is enough to make your body turn off the labour until you feel relaxed again.' She looked around and they were all engrossed in her words. 'Your fight-or-flight hormone overriding your labour-inducing hormone.'

Poppy stopped for a moment to let that sink in. She pointed to week four on the schedule sheet. 'Which is why we include a tour of the birthing rooms and encourage you to bring your own things from home when you do go into labour. Make your own nests in the hospital.'

After the class, Jake was quiet as they drove home. Poppy looked across at his face a couple of times to see his expression, but it was too hard to tell in the passing streetlights. She really had wanted him to get something out of the evening.

'Because you're a doctor, I suppose it must have been pretty boring for you tonight?' Poppy couldn't stand the suspense any longer. The negative comment surprised her as it came out, but it got right up Jake's nose.

'So, because I'm a doctor, I can't get excited about my own baby's growth and development? Or how to help the mother of my child stay relaxed in labour?'

Poppy shook her head in the dark but he cut her

off before she could speak. Jake pulled over to the side of the road and turned to face her.

'Because I'm a doctor—like your first husband was?' The bitterness in Jake's voice shook Poppy, and she realised just how many of Tyson's sins she'd visited on Jake.

'I'm trying really hard here, Poppy, and I'm beginning to think it's a one-way street. How long does it take you to trust me? Let me get involved. Tell me your problems. I'm giving you space but don't shut me out.'

'Jake, I'm sorry. You're right.' Poppy bit her lip.

His voice softened. 'I don't want answers tonight, honey. I just want you to think about it. Think about what you know of me and don't compare me to the other guy. OK?' He leaned across and kissed her forehead. 'I need you to trust me. Our baby needs you to trust me. Believe that you're very important to me and not just because you're carrying our child.'

He kissed her goodbye at her door. Poppy stared into the darkness long after his taillights had gone. But he hadn't said he loved her.

Maybe she was being unfair to Jake. It had been a pretty stupid thing to assume he would be 'above' the antenatal classes. She was a midwife and learned something new each time she ran one. Now that her own labour was drawing nearer, the information became even more fascinating. Of course Jake would gain, too. She bit her lip. They needed to talk about her expectations for labour as well.

It had been a busy week at work. Today had been frantic and Poppy's back hurt from helping at the last labour. The young mother had wanted to have her baby on the mat on the floor, supported by her husband and the midwife.

It had all worked out well but Poppy's own ligaments were loose from pregnancy and easily overstretched. Even though she'd been reasonably comfortable, sitting on her heels beside the woman, the strain of leaning down to check the progress of the labour, as well as helping to support the mother when she squatted, had taken its toll. She was annoyed with herself for not being more careful.

She was easing herself gingerly onto her motor scooter just as Jake pulled up beside her. He slammed the door of his car and Poppy looked up, surprised. Jake never slammed doors. He marched over to her.

He stopped and towered in front of her with his arms crossed over his chest. 'Are you OK?' Poppy heard the censure in his voice and it was the last straw. She knew she'd been stupid—she didn't need him to tell her.

'Fine, thanks. Don't start.'

Jake raised his eyebrows. 'Don't start about the fact that you're hobbling like an old woman? Or don't start about the fact that you're still riding a scooter at thirty four weeks?'

His face was serious but then she saw the smile in his eyes and sighed in relief. 'OK. You're right. I am sore and I don't feel like riding my bike home. And I hate it when you're right.' She looked up at him and glared. 'Why wouldn't I be miserable?'

He held out his hand for the helmet she hadn't put on.

'Give it to me. I'll ride your embarrassingly small bike home for you and you can take my car.'

Poppy felt the laughter bubble up like a shaken can of cola. It spluttered out of her and she held her stomach as she laughed. He was gorgeous.

'You can't ride that. The conservative Dr Sheppard? What if someone saw you?' She giggled again. 'Besides, you don't have a licence.'

'Little do you know, woman.' He flipped open his wallet. 'I was a temporary Australian in my youth. I had a road bike and still have my licence.' He pointed to the motorbike classification. 'So don't ding my car.'

Jake dropped his keys into her hand and pulled the tight helmet on. His large frame concertinaed onto the little bike, with his knees barely fitting behind the windshield. He puttered down the street with only a slight wobble after take-off and Poppy stared after him, hiccuping.

By the time she'd parked his car carefully against the kerb outside her house the bath water was running. Jake was rummaging through her aromatherapy oils, looking for something to put in the water.

'Two drops of lavender will do me. You have to be careful with oils during pregnancy.' She sighed at the thought of a hot bath and his thoughtfulness. 'It'll relax me and that'll help my back.' She watched him carefully count the drops. Then he put the lid back on. Tyson would never have done that.

'Who are you and where is the conservative Dr Sheppard? What have you done with him?' Poppy teased this man who, she was coming to realise, had accepted a lot in the last few months. 'You're pretty wonderful, you know, Jake.'

He turned to face her and put his arms around her shoulders to look into her eyes. 'I happen to think you're pretty wonderful yourself, Ms McCrae. So how about you slide your delectably rounded body into that bath and I'll whip up a nice cold glass of juice to give you energy?' He left her.

Poppy stared at the empty doorway, feeling confused. If her body was so delectable, how come he didn't stay and watch? She shook her head. It was getting so she wanted him with her more and more. She dropped her clothes on the floor and climbed awkwardly into the bath.

The water lapped gently against her breasts as she sank as low as she could, and the aroma of the lavender made her sigh. She closed her eyes and felt the tension loosening from her shoulders.

'Don't go to sleep in there.' Jake put the juice down on the chair beside the bath. 'I have to go back to work but I'll come back later after you've had a sleep. Maybe you'll have even restored your sunny disposition back to its usual unpredictability.'

She spoke without opening her eyes. 'That's a big word. I'm feeling nice and relaxed. See you.' She opened her eyes. 'Thanks, Jake.' She meant it.

Much later that evening they sat sipping juice on the verandah. Jake had brought takeaway Chinese and they'd eaten out of the plastic containers.

'MSG-free, for our child.' Jake looked proud he'd

thought of it. 'I've just had another scarier thought. It's only a few weeks until the baby's due.'

He swivelled around to stare at Poppy. 'How do you feel about that? Does the labour scare you? It sure as hell scares me and I only have to watch.'

'Don't worry, Jake. You'll be doing more than watching. You have to rub my back, be there to lean on, support me when I go through the turbulent time of transition and want to go home, get in the shower with me.' Poppy smiled dreamily.

'It's natural. Remember that. A woman's body is designed to bear children and I want to listen to my body as it tells me how to do it.'

'Sounds like you don't need a doctor at all.' Jake was joking.

Poppy wasn't. She looked sideways at him and drew a deep breath.

'I don't. I've booked into my own ward and planned on a totally natural birth. A midwife will be there to assist if she's needed with the actual birth and I'll go home soon after. I'm doing this on my own. With your help.'

Jake sat bolt upright. 'What about medical back-up?'

She sighed. 'In a perfect world, I would have liked a home birth, with you as the *accoucheur*.' She smiled gently as his mouth dropped open. 'But I can do the next best thing, and I'm doing this for you, Jake—it's not my choice. I'll have our baby in a birthing unit. If I need help, we'll call them. But I'm not going to need help.'

His throat worked. 'You are going to a doctor for your antenatal visits, aren't you?'

'I went once, for the first visit. But Sandy's looking after my antenatal care. She used to be an independent home-birth midwife. I'll bet my antenatal care is as good as, if not better than, any obstetrician would give. If I had a high-risk pregnancy, it would be different and I'd have to see an obstetrician, but I don't. Haven't you read the slogan on my car? ''Start Life with a Midwife.'''

Jake ran his hands through his hair and took a couple of deep breaths. He spoke his thoughts out loud. 'This is too much. But I don't really have any say in this, do I, Poppy?'

He paced the verandah and stared over the verandah gripping the rail. After a few minutes she saw his shoulders loosen and he turned back to face her.

'You will be in hospital?' She nodded her head. 'Why didn't I think of all this?' He rubbed his forehead. 'I should have known it wasn't going to be conventional.'

He held up his hands. 'Give me some time to get used to it. You're the person who has to do it. I appreciate you're trying to meet me halfway here. But I was brought up as a wait-for-the-doctor kind of person.' He stood up. 'I think I might head home.'

Poppy stood up, too. Her cheeks dimpled cheekily. 'You took it better than I thought you might.' She kissed him. 'Don't be angry with Sandy. She wasn't allowed to tell you. She's terrified you'll be wild with her.'

He lowered his brows at her. 'The things your friends do for you. Wait until I see her.' Then he smiled and she knew it was all right. 'I'll catch you tomorrow at work or else I'll see you at the beach on Sunday. Do you want me to pick you and the boys up, or are you going in your car?'

'I'll take mine, thanks.' Poppy always took hers.

'Why am I not surprised?' There was a tinge of bitterness in Jake's comment, but he only shrugged philosophically and left.

CHAPTER NINE

IT WAS Sunday, and Poppy was really starting to begrudge the extra weight as she trudged through the sand to her favourite spot. She realised the flags had been moved further up the beach today, but she wasn't swimming anyway—she looked like a whale now she had only a month to go. She huffed and puffed as she walked and every now and then heard herself wheezing as she breathed out. 'Stinking asthma.'

'What?' Simon asked his aunt as he sat on the towel beside her.

'Beg your pardon,' corrected Poppy automatically. 'Don't say "what".' She hoped he would forget the question.

'Beg your pardon, Auntie Pop?' His bright green eyes didn't look at all confused. Poppy sighed.

'I've got a cold, Simon, and I'm cranky about it.' She ruffled his red hair and hugged him to her. He was so cute.

'Can I go down and build a sandcastle at the edge of the waves with Aidan's GI Joe?'

'OK, sweetheart, but don't go in the water. I'll watch you.' She watched him scamper down to the edge of the sea, his yellow shorts and tiny orange shirt vivid in the sun. The Nippers were further along the beach and she could see Jake organising them into relay teams. A jogger was trotting her way and she recognised Daniel.

Simon perched GI Joe on top of the mound. The waves lapped the edge of his castle and retreated. He laughed in delight. He pushed a mound out of the sand a bit closer to the edge. The next wave came in and swirled around GI Joe, wetting the plastic boots on the action man's feet. Simon laughed again. He didn't see a big wave coming and it snatched GI Joe and tossed the figure into the surf. Simon straightened out of his crouch and looked up at Auntie Pop. She was talking to a man. He'd better not interrupt.

He pulled the edges of his shorts up with his fingers and followed the wave as it dragged GI Joe into the water.

'Hi, Daniel. How're you enjoying being a father? How's Debbie and the baby?'

The young man's face lit up. 'Great, everyone's great. I still run on the beach every day, but it depends on Rory what time I get away. Kids sure change your life.'

Poppy laughed and shooed him on his way. 'Don't waste that precious time. Say hello to Deb for me.'

She was still smiling about his comment on children changing one's life when she looked up to check on Simon. He wasn't there. She swivelled her head and scanned the children playing at sandcastles further along, but couldn't see his orange shirt. She heaved herself to her feet and bit back a moan of panic.

'Simon?' She looked out to sea and saw the tiny orange flash as he rolled over and was dragged behind a wave. *'Simon!'*

Jake was having trouble concentrating. The children were skittish and Poppy was sitting on a mound at the periphery of his vision. He caught a movement out of the corner of his eye and couldn't believe what he was seeing. Poppy was running awkwardly down the slope to the water, pulling off her shirt as she ran, her stomach poking out in front of her.

He looked in the direction she was running but couldn't see anything. 'Keep them out of the water and take over.' He fired the order over his shoulder to the trainee lifesaver, and loped towards Poppy as she splashed through the waves out to the deeper water. She struck out through the waves as if she were possessed by a demon, and Jake felt the fear settle in his chest as he saw a brief flash of orange roll over in the waves. Simon.

Poppy reached Simon as Jake grabbed a surfboard from a passing teenager and paddled towards them. She was breathing hard as she reached her nephew, who was face down. Treading water, she spun him face up then blew a mouthful of air into his lungs, submerging herself in the process. She wasn't able to do anything about his breathing on her own so she kicked hard and came up for air, trying for backstroke and changing her hold until she had his body almost lying across her stomach.

'Hold on, Simon. Come on.' She panted and gave up talking, needing her breath.

'Poppy!' Jake's voice couldn't have sounded any more welcome. The nose of the surfboard skimmed past her shoulder. 'Hang onto the board—I'll take him now.'

Poppy grabbed at the edge of the board as Jake lifted Simon onto it. She grabbed the boy's arm and concentrated on trying to feel the faint beat in his tiny wrist.

'He's got a pulse.' Now that they had a surface to work on, Jake was able to puff air into the child's lungs, and Poppy could see the rise and fall of Simon's chest. The hand she was holding suddenly twitched, and Simon coughed to get rid of the sea water in his lungs.

Poppy let go of his arm and held onto the board with both hands, resting her cheek against it. Her breathing was half sob and half gasp. She was too breathless to cry.

Another two boards arrived with lifeguards, and one offered her a ride back to the shore. She nodded, hoping she could get away before Jake realised how breathless she was.

There was a crowd of onlookers on the beach, and as Poppy reached the shore Samuel and Aidan ran up to her and flung themselves against her. She staggered back a step and held up her hand as she tried to catch her breath. It was all too much. She dragged some air into her lungs and wasted it talking.

'He's OK. Jake's with him.' She put her hands on her hips and sucked in as much air as she could. 'Samuel, grab my bag and towel, please. I need my bag.' Samuel took off and Poppy sank to her knees on the sand.

Aidan sounded more confident that all would be well now. 'Someone said they called an ambulance.'

Poppy was glad. The sooner Simon was monitored in hospital, the safer he'd be. Salt-water immersion could have delayed complications. How was she going to tell her sister she'd nearly allowed Simon to drown?

Samuel skidded to a halt beside her and she rummaged through her bag until her hand felt the puffer of Ventolin. She put it to her mouth and puffed several times. As she took it away from her mouth she looked up and saw Jake.

His face looked as if it were carved from stone, implacable. The voice he used when he spoke sounded like a stranger's.

'You have asthma.' It was statement. 'You didn't think I needed to know.' He shook his head in disgust. She saw him take a deep breath before he asked, 'Are you all right?'

'Yes.'

She saw a flash of despair in his eyes before they went blank again.

'I'll go with Simon in the ambulance. Do you want me to ring his mother?'

Poppy shook her head. 'I'll do it.' She wheezed.

'Goodbye, Poppy.' He turned and walked away.

Simon was in hospital for three days and Jake treated Poppy as if she had the plague. The day Simon came out of hospital Jake left town. Poppy was at home when he rang.

'Poppy?'

'Jake!'

'Simon's going home today. I just rang to say he'd be fine. You did a great job to get to him so quickly.'

'I couldn't have done it without you.' She bit her lip. 'Jake—I need to see you.'

'I don't think so. I'm going away for a few days.' His voice was distant. 'You don't need me, Poppy. Look after yourself because you sure as hell won't let me.' Then he hung up.

Poppy's chest hurt. She sank onto the lounge and put her feet up on a pillow.

She'd finally done it. She'd driven Jake away. Maybe it was time to rethink what she really wanted. In her heart she knew she loved him. Not in the way she'd been bowled over by Tyson's smoothness. This was a warts-and-all kind of love. And he'd certainly taken her on like that.

She knew Jake could be autocratic and domineering—but mainly when he was worried about her. He was incredibly conservative but then she'd thrown his proposal of marriage back in his conventional face, denying him the right to legally acknowledge his child and forcing him to acknowledge an illegitimate liaison. Which he had. Unflinchingly.

She'd called him dogmatic but he'd stood up for her to Tyson and had adapted to her house. In fact, he'd accepted the differences between them graciously. Had she? Did she really think that Jake would belittle her beliefs now that she knew him better?

Poppy took a long, hard look at herself and didn't like what she saw. What about her? She'd demanded a midwife delivery when she'd known Jake would have been more comfortable with at least Dr Gates present. Also she'd kept him at arm's length and had thrown him out of her house when she hadn't liked what he'd said. She'd even assumed he'd be bored at her antenatal class and hadn't told him about her asthma when he'd asked about her health.

Really, she hadn't given him any benefit of the doubt.

She had tried and convicted him of being untrustworthy—like Tyson. No wonder he'd finally taken all he could.

She wiped away the tears that had fallen on her stomach. 'Sorry, baby. I'm making you all wet.' She caressed her stomach, the pain in her heart more wrenching as she saw what she'd lost for both of them.

'It was all there. Jake would have been a wonderful husband and father, but I was so afraid of doing the wrong thing that I forgot how to live.'

That night was the last of the antenatal classes. Poppy drove herself in and missed Jake's company badly. It had become such a routine for him to drive her in, do the class with her and then come back to her house for a late supper.

'Hi, Poppy. Where's Jake?' Every person she greeted as they came into class seemed to ask the same question. She didn't know how much more she could stand without bursting into tears.

'He's away.' She smiled brightly at a late arrival and gestured for them to leave the cake on the table. 'I see you all remembered it's party night. We've got a guest speaker from Women's Health to discuss contraception first.' As usual they all laughed at the thought of contraception being necessary after nine months of not worrying about it. 'And then we can all sit around and gorge ourselves silly and have a question time.'

Katrina, the note-taker, stood up and pulled a bunch of flowers out from behind her back. 'Before we start, Poppy, we all pitched in and wanted to give you these. We really enjoyed the classes and I, for one, feel much more confident about labour and being a mother after the last eight weeks.'

Poppy squeezed her lips together, frantically trying not to cry, but the tears slipped out and down her face. She sniffed and looked up at the people who'd become friends over the last two months then smiled wryly.

'Well, isn't it lucky you guys know all about hormone changes in pregnancy and people suddenly starting to cry?' She wiped her eyes with her hand. 'Thanks. You've been a great class and I might even meet some of you when we go in to have our babies. If you see me in labour, don't forget to tell me to relax.' They all crowded around her and one of the men pushed a brown package into her hand.

'We bought Jake a cigar. Can you give it to him from us, please?'

Poppy smiled and nodded, but didn't even try to speak through her tight throat. Luckily, the Women's Health nurse arrived for her talk, and

Poppy ushered her up to the front of the room. Not surprisingly, her introduction was quick and not as distinct as usual. Poppy slipped from the room to get herself a drink of water and leaned her shoulder against the wall in the privacy of the kitchen.

This was too much. The class had appreciated how great Jake was. She had to find Jake and make him understand that she loved him. That she was willing to be an equal partner, to give and not just take in the trust department. But was it too late?

What was she going to do about it? She didn't even know where he'd gone. The rumours, and there were always rumours in a hospital, said that Jake's father was sick again, but Poppy found out that wasn't true.

CHAPTER TEN

JAKE wasn't with his parents—because they were in Midcoast! When Poppy answered the door she knew straight away who they were.

His mother was smaller than she'd imagined and his father taller, but she could see Jake in both of them. They were expensively dressed. Mrs Sheppard's silver hair was immaculately coiffured. Poppy wore a sarong, with her belly pushing it open. Daunting to say the least.

'Poppy McCrae?' Jake's mother spoke precisely. Poppy nodded. 'And you're Dr and Mrs Sheppard. Would you like to come in?'

'My husband is going for a drive but I would like a chance to talk with you if you have the time.'

Poppy looked at the older version of Jake and saw a familiar twinkle in his eye. She couldn't help but smile at him.

'I won't be too long.' He said it ambiguously and waved as he walked down the path. Poppy felt that the only friend she had in the world had just left. She turned back to the small dragon in front of her.

Poppy stepped aside to allow Jake's mother into the room. When she caught up with her she was surprised to see her smiling at the decor.

'I had a college room just like this before I met Jake's father. But we aren't here to talk about me.'

Poppy grimaced to herself and led the way into

the dining room. She decided she needed a table between them and not just a lounge chair.

'Would you like coffee or tea, Mrs Sheppard?' The woman reminded her of her old headmistress.

'Call me Lillian. Perhaps, when my husband returns, but I really don't want to waste time.' She sat at the table and Poppy hovered for a moment before she, too, sat. 'Why won't you marry my son?'

Poppy blinked. That was up front. 'Why do you want me to marry your son?'

'Apart from legitimising my grandchild, it has nothing to do with me whom he marries, but I will tell you this. After his wife died I gave up hoping he would marry again—let alone give me a grandchild.' She stared straight at Poppy. 'You woke him up, made him human again, and he says he loves you. So why won't you marry him?' She shook her head as if she couldn't believe that any woman wouldn't want to marry her son.

Poppy was struggling for reality. 'We're totally different.' It wasn't brilliant but she heaved a sigh of relief that something had come out of her mouth.

'Good. You won't get bored. Give me a better reason.'

Poppy shifted on the chair and the baby kicked. She put her hand on the spot, looked down and smiled at the bump under her sarong. When she looked back across the table she was surprised to see a softness she wouldn't have believed possible on the face of the older woman.

'Do you love him, Poppy?' The words were spoken gently and Poppy felt tears prick the corners of her eyes.

'Yes, but I thought I loved my first husband, too.' She looked up into the face of Jake's mother and there was no condemnation there for her previous marriage.

'Jake told us about him. My son isn't like that. He's totally trustworthy and serious—sometimes too serious. I've been trying to lighten him up for two years.' The autocratic tone was back in her voice.

Poppy saw the change in the lined face across from her. Lillian seemed to age before her eyes.

'I saw the difference your mother made to James in the last few weeks of his life. I know Jake was against him coming here, but I owe your mother a debt of gratitude. We all accepted that James didn't have long to live—except Jake. I never begrudged James the time to come to terms with his illness. He was a different man after he'd been here and, I believe, because of that he died peacefully. And now I see the difference you've made in Jake and I welcome it.'

Despite the pain the older woman had to be feeling, the sincerity on her face touched Poppy.

'Jake took his brother's death hard, as did we all. But following so closely on the heels of losing his wife and unborn child—'

Poppy's indrawn breath stopped the sentence.

'You didn't know she was sixteen weeks pregnant? Did he tell you how she died?'

Poppy shook her head and Lillian went on, 'Jake was in Brisbane overnight at a paediatric conference and Helen was in their house in Sydney. She had an asthma attack and they found her beside the phone.

When he couldn't get an answer from his calls he had his brother check on her. It was too late.'

Poppy closed her eyes. The room was spinning and she felt sick. What had she done to Jake? To find out about her asthma like that. Poor Jake. Poor Helen and baby. She took a deep breath and opened her eyes. Lillian had her head bowed.

'She didn't make him happy, you know.' The older woman stared at the tablecloth. 'There was no spark. She was like a Dresden doll that needed cosseting, and Jake was busy building up his practice. I never saw them laugh together.' She looked up at Poppy. 'Isn't that tragic? Do you laugh together?'

Poppy thought of Jake scrunched up on her motorbike, sniffing her dressing-gown, laughing across the table at the restaurant. She smiled at Lillian. 'Yes, we laugh.' The older woman smiled back.

'So when are you going to marry my son?'

Poppy sat back and laughed out loud. 'You're a scheming woman!'

'Yes, but my husband liked you immediately, and I have great faith in his judgement.'

Lillian looked quite proud of herself and Poppy hated to disillusion her. She looked at her hands and searched for the right words.

'I'm afraid Jake and I aren't communicating at the moment.' When she looked up, Lillian didn't seem surprised.

'Yes, but when you are "communicating" again...' Lillian winked '...do us all a favour and think about putting the poor fellow out of his misery and marrying him. I look forward to welcoming you into the family.'

There was a knock at the door and Lillian stood up. 'My husband. His timing is impeccable. We'll have a cup of tea another day, dear. You may kiss my cheek.' She proffered a powdered cheek and Poppy dutifully kissed it. Her brain was whirling as she escorted her apparently future mother-in-law to the door, still not quite sure what she'd agreed to.

Jake's father stood outside and smiled understandingly at Poppy's obvious bemusement.

'Welcome to the family, my dear. We'll see you soon.'

Poppy watched them drive away in a black Mercedes Benz. Jake's mother stared straight ahead and Jake's father waved. Poppy blinked a few times then slowly turned and walked back into the house. That had been incredible. She felt as if someone had spun her around with a blindfold on and she didn't know which direction she was facing.

At the beach, the look on Jake's face had been one of betrayal. Now she knew why. She hadn't kept her end of the bargain and met him halfway. She hadn't told him her problems and shared her worries with him about her health. Instead, she'd gone to some breathing classes. He did have a right to know. And a right to be worried.

Jake couldn't believe Poppy hadn't told him. He'd been kept on the outside again. He needed uninterrupted decision-making time, without Poppy's presence tilting him off balance.

He was fighting for their love. He believed she loved him—had to believe it. What he didn't know was if that love was strong enough to risk a second failure. She had to meet him halfway or it wasn't going to work.

Jake turned his car north on the Pacific Highway, suddenly realising he hadn't booked accommodation anywhere—very unlike the usually organised and efficient Dr Sheppard. He'd try for one of those resorts in Coffs Harbour.

Then his eye was caught by a large brown billboard at the side of the road. It advertised a motel looking out over the edge of the Dorrigo Plateau all the way to the sea. He swung off the highway and up the winding road to the plateau. The valley dropped spectacularly away below him, and when he reached the mountaintop the blue of the Pacific Ocean shone clearly on the horizon. Well, this was certainly giving him distance.

When he woke on Wednesday morning he drove down to Bellingen. He wasn't ready for soul-searching yet and the place had looked attractive as he'd driven past the evening before. He could feel the corners of his mouth twitch as he walked along the street. He had unwittingly arrived in a town that specialised in alternative therapies and holistic medicine.

He glanced up at the sky. Someone up there was laughing at him. This place was culturally amazing. The most beautiful quartz wind chime he had ever seen caught his eye. Not that he had ever looked out for them before. It hung down for at least three feet and the sheared slice of pink quartz spun gently as the sunlight caught the ragged crystal edges at its centre. It had Poppy written all over it.

He entered the shop for a closer look and the scent

of lavender in the air reminded him of Poppy's house. He smiled at the sarong-clad teenager.

'Are you burning lavender oil?'

'No, the reflexologist has appointments today and his last client was pregnant. He really only likes to use oil with lavender for the pregnant ladies.'

'Reflexology? Is that massage of the feet to stimulate certain areas of the body?' Jake had heard of it but had never met anybody who practised it.

A lilac curtain of beads swished open at the back of the shop and a short, bald man answered for her.

'Not just the feet are used in reflexology. The meridians of the body run from the scalp down to the feet. So an area of the head corresponds with one on the hands and the feet. I usually work on the feet. Are you interested in trying it?'

It was the last thing Jake had thought of trying but he was intrigued by the thought of a pregnant woman coming to see this man. Maybe Poppy saw a reflexologist—he'd be the last to know. He stamped down on the bitterness and tried to open his mind.

'I'm interested in how it works.' That was as close as Jake could go and still tell the truth.

The man grinned and gestured Jake through to a small back room. There was a batik-covered massage table in the centre of the room. The walls were covered in charts depicting areas of the feet that corresponded with areas on the body. Jake fingered the collar of his shirt. He didn't know whether he really wanted to do this.

The next hour was one of the most unusual Jake had ever spent. He wasn't sure how, but he'd signed up for a crash course the next day that would show him the correct techniques for simple massage and basic reflexology. He couldn't believe it. As he passed through the shop he caught sight of the wind chime. Why not?

'I'll have the quartz mobile in the window, please.'

The young girl in the shop smiled shyly and lifted it off the rail. She folded it carefully into a tissue-lined box.

'Rose quartz. It creates harmony, opens the heart to love and releases past emotional pain.'

Jake stared. How could he have picked that one? Maybe they all did it. 'Are there any other stones that do that?'

The girl shrugged. 'They all help to create an environment for different emotions. This is the love stone.' She finished tying a light pink ribbon around the box. 'It's also good for aching bones, eyesight, prevents wrinkles—'

Jake held up his hand and grinned. 'Enough. I'm buying it, OK?'

She handed him the box.

'Thanks.' He walked towards the door, holding the beautifully wrapped box gingerly.

'Oh, one more thing.' The girl was obviously determined that he appreciate the stone.

Jake raised one eyebrow and looked back.

'It's helpful for asthma.'

Jake froze. 'You're kidding?'

The girl shook her head. 'It's true. It's all on the card inside. Good luck with it.'

CHAPTER ELEVEN

FRIDAY morning arrived and Poppy still didn't know where Jake was. The last two days had crawled by and she was miserable. The baby didn't seem to be moving as much either and she felt as though even her child was disappointed in her.

She'd finished work and Sandy was on night duty so she couldn't ring her and talk about her fears that she'd blown her chance with Jake.

Jasmine and Glen had gone to visit Glen's parents with the boys now that Simon was out of hospital. Her sister had understood how quickly children could get into trouble and hadn't blamed her, but Poppy knew she would never forget the frantic fear of that day. Thank God Jake had been there.

She needed him now, too. Where was he? There was so much she had to say to him.

Later that afternoon, when Poppy opened the door to see Jake standing there, she couldn't say a word. Where were all the things she wanted to say, owed it to Jake to say? No words would form. He looked so tall and solid and she felt like he'd been gone for a month not just a few days. She stepped into his arms and her body settled immediately into the niche his body created for her, despite the 'football' out in front. She was home.

'I missed you, Jake.' The incredible thing about

saying those words was how liberated she really felt. He had a right to know she'd missed him. She had a right not to feel threatened by allowing herself to care so much.

'Now, lady, you and I need to settle this once and for all.' He stepped into the house, hugged her fiercely and briefly against him once more, before propelling her into the lounge room.

'I'll talk and you'll listen. When I'm finished, you talk and I'll listen.' Poppy held back the tears. He was being autocratic again and she didn't mind one bit.

Still holding her shoulders, he nudged her into the chair and crouched down in front of her, sliding his hands down her arms until he held both her small hands in his large ones. It felt so good.

'Ah, Poppy. You're killing me slowly. The time has come for you to choose between self-sufficiency and a real family. I'll ask you one more time…' He squeezed her hands. 'Be my wife, in all ways.' He let go of her hands and tapped her chin gently with his finger. 'That includes *communicating*—' he stressed the word '—with your husband and even discussing any concerns you may have about your life or that of our child.'

The bulge of Poppy's stomach moved and rolled with his words and they both smiled. Jake caressed the material over her stomach. Then he looked back into her eyes.

'On my side, I'll communicate with you and promise to admire you for the differences in our beliefs and support you in your efforts to offer holistic midwifery to your clients and with the birth of our child.' The planes of his face stilled as he became even more serious.

'And, finally, I want you to know that I love you, and even if you weren't having my baby, I would want to spend the rest of my life with you.' He dropped a kiss on her nose. 'That's what I wanted to say. Your turn.'

Poppy drew a deep breath but the smile inside her unfurled like a huge flower as she appreciated that all her fears were unfounded. Jake still wanted her. Still loved her.

'I love you, Jake.' She smiled mistily at the strong yet serious face in front of her.

'Thank you for still wanting to be with me when it took me so long to realise that was what I wanted, too. I'm not giving up my independence so much as making my world a bigger place.' She watched the relief cross his face as her words sank in. 'I trust you with my life and that of our baby, and I never thought I'd be able to say that to any man.' She leaned forward and kissed him gently on the lips.

'As for the birth of our baby, it has to be a positive experience for all of us, not just me. If you would prefer Dr Gates to be there, we'll do it. I don't care if there are ten doctors there as long as *you* are.'

She spoke the next sentence slowly and clearly. 'So, yes, please. I'd be honoured to be your wife. For keeps.'

'Yes!'

Jake jumped up and pumped his fist in the air, and Poppy marvelled at the serious Dr Sheppard cavorting like a teenager.

'OK. We have to introduce you to my parents. I've told them all about you.' He looked down at Poppy and pulled her up out of the lounge and into his arms. 'You're not going to be nervous about meeting them, are you?'

Poppy started to laugh. 'I've already had the pleasure of meeting your formidable mother. I'm afraid they've both already welcomed me into your family. You're lucky you decided to marry me because I wouldn't have liked to be the one to tell her we weren't getting married.'

Jake groaned and then laughed. 'What did she say?'

'Lillian found it difficult to understand why any woman wouldn't want to marry her son!'

Jake nodded his head. 'I would have to agree with her.'

Poppy punched him in the arm. 'Conceited man.' Then she wrapped her arms around his waist and leaned against him. 'Though…I have to agree with her, too.'

Three weeks later Poppy was watching the man she loved as he slept. His lips were curved in a small smile and he snored very slightly. She'd have to get him onto the relaxed breathing techniques she was using for her asthma. They were good for that. The pain came again.

'Jake?'

She watched the changes in his face as her voice drifted into his dream. He blinked and opened his eyes.

'Hmm?'

'I think today is your child's birthday.'

He sat bolt upright. 'OK, OK. I'm up.' He swung his feet to the side of the bed and stood there as if he couldn't remember why.

The light went on and Poppy shielded her eyes. He turned it down with the dimmer and smiled sheepishly at her. 'Sorry. I panicked for a minute there, but I'm awake now.' He took a deep breath. 'OK. We have loads of time and we need to stay relaxed.'

Poppy smiled at her flustered husband. 'I am relaxed. Dr Sheppard? Please, remember this is an everyday occurrence in nature.' She winced as the next contraction took her by surprise. She breathed through it quietly and then heaved herself out of the bed when it finished.

'Can I do anything for you?' Jake smiled and hugged her. 'I'm calm. I'll just put your bag in the car and make a cup of tea while you have a shower.'

That sounded wonderful. Poppy leaned against the shower-cubicle wall with the hand shower aimed below her belly button and lower. The hot needles of water diffused the pain just as she'd described in antenatal classes.

Crikey, the pains were strong. She breathed in slowly and deeply through her mouth and visualised her cervix stretching with the pain. Stretching. Pulling up into the body of the uterus and opening. Stretching and opening. The words swirled around her brain with the pain and she felt the baby move as the contraction faded away.

'I'll bet the room is getting smaller inside there, young Sheppard. Whew. Your mother is definitely going to be a better antenatal teacher after you're born.' She grimaced wryly and frowned as the pain started again. And then another one. This was happening too fast.

The next contraction seemed to go on and on until she found herself puffing the breaths in and out. At the height of the contraction she felt the pop of her waters breaking, and she knew the baby wasn't far away. How many times had she told her classes how rare it was for a first-time mother to have a fast labour? She remembered Debbie. Wrong again.

'Jake!'

Jake's head appeared around the shower screen. 'Do you want me to rub your back?'

She shook her head. 'Too late for that.' She met his eyes. 'I felt like pushing with that last pain.'

'You're kidding.' His face paled as she started to breathe through the next contraction, and he could see that she hadn't been kidding. He bit his lip and then seemed to come to a decision. 'You don't want to try climbing into the car?'

Poppy closed her eyes as the pain increased. When it receded she could see the reflection of it in his eyes. 'I could try.' It was the last thing she wanted to do but she would try.

'It's all right, sweetheart. Let's have our baby at home. Shall I ring Sandy?'

'She's still on night duty. She can't leave the ward.'

Jake closed his eyes briefly and then opened them. He smiled gently and his voice was calm. 'Do you want to stay there or do you want to move into the bedroom?'

'Can I have some pillows and a quilt in here in the corner?' Thank God her mother had built the bathroom big!

'Sure. At the restaurant, you said you had an emergency pack somewhere?'

'It's in that drawer in the cabinet.' She watched Jake pull open the drawer and lift out a parcel wrapped in white paper. She knew he'd accepted that it was just the two of them and had dealt with it. She loved him so much. 'It's all sterile.'

Poppy didn't watch Jake set out the clamps for the cord and arrange the bed—she was too busy. She had time for a smile when she heard the relaxation music start, and concentrated on obeying the commands of her body. The feeling of urgency and slight panic faded, and she realised she'd passed transition. Her body slowed its frenetic pace and she sensed the change with a clarity that thrilled her.

Jake came back into the room with a small bundle of the new facecloths she'd washed for the baby and a bunny rug. 'Anything else?' He didn't look flustered and she felt humbled by his ability to deal with something he must have thought he'd been safe from.

She stepped quickly from the shower as she felt the rolling tightness of the next pain. She leaned her elbows on the bath edge and knelt on a towel he'd placed to save her knees. 'You know, you're a wonderful man.' She looked into his eyes. 'Just hold me.' The big picture window beside the bath looked out into the trees and she focussed on a star in the night sky visible through the foliage.

Jake clasped her shoulders and pulled his body

into line with hers, and they worked through the next contractions together. She sighed.

'Soon,' she panted, and leaned away from the bath to wriggle back into a sitting position against the pillows, so that she'd be able to see and feel her baby's head when it was born.

Jake had taken the bathroom mirror off its hook on the wall and propped it in the corner. He adjusted the angle so that Poppy could see what was happening.

He watched her concentrating with the next pain, and felt the tightness of emotion in his chest as the downy hair of the baby's head appeared for the first time.

'Can you see him, Poppy?' Jake whispered, awed at the birth of his own child, although he'd been present at hundreds of labour ward births and Caesareans.

'Could be a girl,' Poppy gasped between pushes, and Jake felt his chest swell with pride. This earth mother was his partner in life and she had never looked so beautiful to him as she trusted in her body to do what was needed. He knew that he would never view medical intervention in a birth in quite the same way again now that he'd witnessed the power of nature.

His baby's head extended, first the back of the head then the forehead appeared at the threshold, and then the nose and mouth appeared until the baby's entire head had been born. Jake couldn't believe that he was the only one here to help. It suddenly hit him. What if something went wrong?

'Check for the cord, Jake.' Poppy's voice sounded

far away, and it was as if a bucket of cold water hit him. Of course he should check to see that the umbilical cord hadn't curled around the baby's head, or it could pull tight as the body was born.

He gently felt around the baby's neck, still inside Poppy, and his heart jumped as he felt the rope-like thickness of the cord lying loosely around the baby's neck. It's OK, it's loose, he calmed himself. Then he curled his fingers over the cord to lift it over the baby's head.

'Thank God,' he heard himself mutter out loud as he watched the baby's head turn as the shoulders rotated to fit under the pelvic arch. The next contraction started, and as Poppy pushed, first one shoulder and then the other appeared until the baby slithered out onto the towel in a final rush. It was a girl.

Jake wiped her little face with a facecloth and she screwed up her face as if to complain about the light. Her little hands clenched and Jake could feel the tears running down his face as he realised that his child was going to be fine.

He stared at Poppy, and the exultant joy on her face as she, too, stared at their daughter brought fresh tears to his face. He lifted the baby gently and placed her against the warmth of Poppy's breasts. The two women he loved most in the world were safe, and he was glad to be alive.

Later, when Poppy and Rose Lillian were tucked up in his bed, Jake stood on the verandah and stared into the night. He wished he could tell his brother his news. The early morning stars winked at him. He felt the load of guilt and remorse fall from his shoulders and he breathed the night air deep into his lungs. James wouldn't have wanted him to dwell on past mistakes. If James hadn't found his way here…

'Thank you, James. For helping me find my life.'

CHAPTER TWELVE

THE bride was dressed in an embroidered white cotton gown and wore yellow roses in her hair. In honour of her mother. The groom wore white trousers and an open necked white shirt with a bright yellow poppy in his buttonhole. In honour of the woman he loved.

'You may kiss the bride.' The minister smiled benevolently at them.

'I introduce to you, Dr and Mrs Sheppard.'

The sun beamed suddenly bright through a gap in the ceiling of the forest to illuminate Poppy and Jake as they greeted their guests. Jake imagined it was his brother directing the light show from heaven. Catching his mother's eye, he could see she was thinking of James, too. The setting was all Poppy had said it would be.

He looked up again into the cathedral-like ceiling of the green rainforest roof canopy before he turned, holding his wife's hand, to the tiny congregation seated on the tree stumps in the clearing. There *was* something particularly poignant about a wedding amongst the trees.

'Poppy, I thought you were mad to want your wedding here.' Jake's mother passed back her chubby granddaughter and looked around. 'Even though I would have preferred Vaucluse House, I must admit it was very beautiful. Welcome to the family, my dear.'

She kissed the baby girl on the forehead. 'Bye, sweetie. Gran will see you at the restaurant.'

She patted Jake on the cheek. 'Congratulations, darling. It's wonderful to see you so happy.' Then she turned to her husband and took his hand. 'Take me out of here, John, before I become eaten by insects.'

Poppy and Jake looked at each other and both started to laugh. They could hear Jake's mother whispering to her husband, 'They do laugh together, John.'

Poppy shifted the chuckling baby to her other shoulder and turned to the man she loved and trusted like no other. Jake took her hand and raised it to his lips, and she could feel the mantle of his love about her like an aura. Poppy finally felt as if she was home.